# ONCE UPON A SCREAM

### Edited by Dan Shaurette

Written in Paris —
once upon a time

See page 167

Love,
Laurel Anne Hill
7/23/16

ONCE UPON A SCREAM

Printed in the United States of America.
Edited by Dan Shaurette
Copy Editor: Larriane Wills
Cover art: Dan Shaurette
Artwork by Yaroslav Gerzhedovich

ISBN: 978-1530529513

HorrorAddicts.net Press
www.horroraddicts.net
HorrorAddicts@gmail.com

*This book is dedicated to
all of our childhood teachers who shared
with us their love for reading and
laid the foundations for our imaginations.*

# CONTENTS

# FOREWORD

There was, once upon a time, a tradition of telling tales with elements of the fantastic along with the frightful. Adults and children alike once took heed not to go into the deep, dark woods, or treat a stranger poorly, or make a deal with someone—or something—without regard for the consequences. Be careful of what you wish for or you just might get it.

For one reason or another, as the tales were told and written down, they became sanitized for our protection. They have become pastiches where everyone lives happily ever after and their dreams come true. They became bedtime stories to tell children to lull them to sleep.

That trend has been bucked many times over the years. Most recently with motion pictures like *Maleficent, Snow White and the Huntsman, Hansel and Gretel: Witch Hunters*, or television shows like *Once Upon A Time* and *Grimm*.

As I watched these new interpretations, I realized I wanted to read an anthology of fairy tales that not only returned to their dark, foreboding roots, but where the horror is front and center. Far from lullabies, I wanted to see nightmares borne in black and white.

I think this collection of stories makes a good stab at fulfilling my wishes. Within these pages you will find familiar fairy tales told with a new darker spirit as well as new stories that still forewarn of lurking horrors. So lock your doors and shutter your windows. Let's find out how happily ever after these tales will end.

*- Dan Shaurette*

# THE BLACK UNDEATH
*by Shannon Lawrence*

*The hideous little man stomped his feet in a bizarre jig, leaping around the room and cackling. Flesh peeled off his right cheek, and he pressed it into place without stopping his momentum. Lady Rebecca shuddered and held her baby closer to her chest. She winced when baby Charlie bit her breast, but didn't release him. The feverish warmth of his little body seeped through the blankets, dimming the cold of the room.*

*The man stopped his cavorting and settled in front of the couple and their baby. Up close, the ravages on his face and body were more visible. Though his shaggy clothes and ragged beard covered what may have been even worse damage, plenty was still evident. The skin not missing in patches was covered with solid scabrous bumps, his lips nothing more than a set of overlapping flesh-colored bumps the size of a woman's fingertip. Black tinged with green crept up his nose and hands, spreading in an uneven line as if he was rotting from the inside out. His blackened fingers were twisted bulbous knobs, terrifying claws that reached toward the baby covetously. The distinctive smell of rot rolled out in front of him, infiltrating her nostrils and coating her tongue. It was all she could do not to squeeze the baby tighter. She didn't want to suffocate him, though she'd considered it a few times since this plague had struck him.*

*Before them, the man wheezed a bit from his exertions, hocking up what appeared to be a glistening red piece of flesh. Rebecca heard her husband, Lord Azrael, gag beside her, a quiet choking, but from the corner of her eye she could see he sat straight and tall, his crown astride his head.*

# ONCE UPON A SCREAM

*The man's voice came out in a strained croak. "This is your final guess, and then that baby of yours stays one of us forever, rotting away, coveting flesh just like the rest of us. Tell me, what is my name?"*

*Rebecca hoped with all of her being her information was correct.*

❧

The Black Death had decimated the population in Europe, wiping out entire towns. Much worse, though, was the plague that followed, the Black Undeath. A combination of bubonic plague and leprosy, thanks to an isolated leper colony that had been hit by the plague. This one didn't kill its victims. They stayed quite alive, rotting from the inside out, becoming increasingly disfigured and mindless, while exhibiting symptoms of both leprosy and the plague. Worst of all, the only thing sustaining them was the flesh of living creatures.

Rather than being spread by trade, as the first plague had been, this one was spread by priests, who traveled from leper colonies to towns, unaware of the infection they carried until the first symptoms showed, sometimes weeks after exposure.

Within weeks of his baptism, baby Charlie had started to shake with chills, his temperature climbing. Rebecca felt helpless as he slept more often, refusing to nurse. One day, three weeks in, he began to convulse, saliva bubbling out of his cupid's bow of a mouth. The village physician declared him possessed by a demon, and Father

Percy was called to their home. When the messenger returned, declaring the priest had refused his admittance and sent word he was sick, Lord Azrael himself grabbed his horse and went to the priest's simple church.

His initial knock on the wooden door was ignored, but he pounded all the more forcefully, trying the door, which was barred. When he slammed his body into the door, a weak voice from inside called, "Do not enter. I am ill, and you do not wish to be so."

"My son is demon possessed, Father. You will take care of him, sick or not. It is making him gravely ill, and we fear he cannot continue to fight it."

The priest's voice was so quiet Azrael had to press his ear to the door in order to hear him. "What is the nature of this possession? What symptoms does he suffer?"

"He shakes and convulses, his eyes rolling back in his head. His head burns with heat. He sleeps always and does not eat."

"Oh, my son, the news is worse or better, as you take it. He is not possessed, but plague-stricken."

"Impossible! Come out here where I may speak to you directly."

A shuffling sounded through the door, faint at first, but growing closer. Azrael heard sniffles, followed by the slide of the wooden bar on the other side. The door swung open, darkness in its place. Blackened fingers wrapped around the rim, and the priest shifted himself around it, his nose black, eyes red-rimmed, a smear of red across his mouth and cheek. A large white growth stood out on his throat, swollen and painful looking, and a gangrenous scent wafted from his body.

"I speak the truth. Your son is ill. Soon, like me, he will crave warm, living flesh as his own disintegrates." He revealed his other hand, which gripped a chicken by the neck. It had clearly been chewed on, its flesh torn and bloody. Azrael looked again at the red stain on the priest's face and backpedaled, drawing his sword.

Rather than show fear, the priest lifted the chicken to his mouth and gnawed, making guttural noises as he did so. He pulled back, feathers sticking to the fresh blood, and gave Azrael a grotesque smile.

"You'll do what you have to, of course. It is as God wills."

He dropped the chicken and stepped through the doorway, spreading his arms to the sky, head thrown back. When his hood slid back, Azrael saw blood coming from his ears, dried in a path down his neck.

Without further hesitation, Azrael stepped forth, and with one stroke cleaved the priest's head from his shoulders. The body dropped to the ground, the head rolling toward Azrael, who backed away through the gate and shut it. A wet thunk sounded on the other side as the priest's oozing head came to rest against it.

Azrael mounted his horse, urging it toward home. There had to be a cure for Charlie, and he would find it.

ॐॐ

*"Ambrocius?" Lady Rebecca asked.*
*A cackle and a slow shake of the head answered.*
*"Persimmon?"*
*"No!"*
*"Percy? Alastair? Charles? Henry? Falstaff? Hector?"*
*"No, no, no, no, no, no!" More cackling and the dry rub of finger nubs. "Keep going. You'll never guess it."*

ॐॐ

The palace messengers were sent far and wide to seek someone who knew of a cure. Though they found no one, someone else did, deep in the night. The lady was awake, snuggling wee Charlie, rubbing his once sweet cheeks and silky hair. His extremities had become black, his throat and groin swollen, and the skin around his nose thickened, beginning to boil over into lumps. She knew not how she and Azrael remained untainted, but it was a blessing she would not question too closely.

She could not sleep, for fear of her baby convulsing, so she was awake when the stranger appeared in the bedroom.

The manor was heavily guarded, their bedchamber more so, but he appeared in silence, one moment not there, the next a dark presence against the still closed door. Her chest squeezed in fear, her pulse pounding. She clutched Charlie, squinting into the gloom.

"Who is there?" she called, her voice trembling.

"I come to help, Milady. Your little one is sick, yes?"

"How come you to know this?"

"Messengers, mum. They travel far, and word spreads."

"Come out of the shadows, show yourself."

The shadows moved around him as he stepped forward, then they pulled back, so slowly it seemed they regretted his loss. His terrifying decayed features stood out to her, and she pulled back, pressing her body into the headboard behind her.

"How can you help when you cannot even help yourself?"

"I choose not to help myself. I like this new way. I know how to help, though, if you would have it."

The little man's smile revealed dark dried blood between his teeth, which were brown and broken, filthy, and askew. Fluid leaked from one eye, which was cloudy and only starting to show white flesh overhanging it. One knobby hand came up to swipe at the liquid sliding down his face, and his grin widened at the look of disgust that overtook Rebecca's face.

"How can you help? Why, if you like it so much?"

"Oh, I extract a price, one way or the other, dear lady."

"And that price?"

"If I should help, you'll pay in gold. If you fail, I get the child." His tongue, gray and cracked, protruded through his lips and swiped dryly across his upper lip.

Rebecca shuddered. "Never!"

"Without this deal, your child becomes a ravening undead beast, never to age, always decaying. He will not return to you."

"Leave here now. I do not wish your kind of help."

The little man nodded, scratching his scalp until pieces of himself littered the ground around his feet. A heavy odor sat about him like a cloak, the cool breeze from the windows wafting it over to Rebecca.

"I will give you some time to consider, but not too much, or it will be too late. You'll see me again in seven days, at which time you decide whether to save your son or sacrifice him."

"Get out!" she screamed.

And he was gone.

∂∘∾

*"I could kill you," Azrael said.*

*The little man merely laughed some more, throwing his head back with glee and doing a miniature version of the previous jig before settling again in front of them.*

*"You could, your lordship, but I am the only chance your son has. Kill me now and we may be done with this. Otherwise, go on. Guess."*

*Rebecca placed a hand, firm yet gentle, on Azrael's shoulder. He sat back, pent-up rage evident in his every move, but he nodded to her, his lips pressed together. She continued.*

*"Perseus? Agamemnon? Randal? John? Berthold?"*

*Giggles, this time, raspy and disturbing, but giggles all the same.*

*"Bertrand? Phillip? Luther?"*

*"No, uh-uh, nope."*

*"Get on with it!" Azrael yelled, his face red, eyes puffy from lack of sleep.*

*Rebecca nodded and took a deep breath.*

☙❧

When next the wizened little man showed in their bedchamber, both lord and lady were awake, desperation having overtaken their every moment. Charlie's features were no longer discernible as much more than pustules, lumps, and shredding flesh. He wouldn't suckle at his mother's breast, instead gumming at her in a raging hunger that could not possibly be sated. To hold him over, they fed him calf's blood, but there was no way it would nourish him forever. Or perhaps it could, but their sanity could not be nourished by the same.

Though they had every wall sconce and candle lit, the little man managed to appear out of nowhere, once again enveloped by shadows.

When she noticed him, Rebecca lacked the energy to even be startled. Instead, she sighed, the long-suffering hopeless sigh of a mother watching her child die, helpless to do anything about it.

"How can you help us?"

Stepping into the light, the little man said, "I can cure him, but there is something you must do first."

Satisfied with letting her husband make any deal necessary, Rebecca withdrew to her chair, eyes only for Charlie.

Beside her, Azrael asked, "That is?"

"You must figure out my name."

"What?"

"Names hold great power, lordship. Once you wield mine, you wield the power I can provide to you. This is not something I can simply give you."

"How are we supposed to find your name?"

"That's up to you. I warn you, though, you have a mere three chances to guess my name. Each visit, you may expend as many names as you please, but there will be only three visits. Failure to come up with my name by the third results in my leaving with yon babe."

"What makes you think I'd let you leave with my son?"

"You will not have a choice."

Azrael stood in anger, fists clenched at his sides, face scarlet. "How dare you dictate to me…"

The little man showed anger for the first time. His speed was great as he launched himself across the room to stand directly in front of Azrael. He seemed to grow taller until his destroyed face was even with the other man's. When he spoke, his voice was deeper, more menacing, though he did not yell.

"Silence. I grow bored with this conversation. You have an entire village's resources at your hands. Surely you can figure out a simple name, mm?"

Azrael stumbled back then caught himself, straightening his spine and sticking out his chest. He dared not regain the steps he had given up, instead standing to his full height where he had ended up.

Oddly, the little man appeared to have returned to his original height, just a tiny desiccated figure in raggedy clothes, stinking of rot and filth. He waited with steady, unblinking calm for an answer.

Rebecca spoke before her husband could. "We accept your terms. How long until your first visit?"

"I see your child sickens quickly. You will see me again in two days."

Then he vanished.

Azrael immediately called for his messengers, sending them out in every direction to ask after the little man.

By the evening of the second day, one-third of the messengers had reported in, the others ordered to stay out longer, to go farther. Azrael was prepared with scrolls of names to read. Sadly, none of these were the right names, and the little man promised to return within two more days.

The second time failed, just as the first had. Charlie's symptoms worsened, and he awoke only long enough to drink the offered calf's blood. His features were unrecognizable; he failed to even look like a baby anymore, save his tiny stature.

Rebecca, though, had noticed something during the little man's last visit. In his tangled beard had been a plant, one which was extremely rare. She knew of only one place deep within the forest where the plant could be found. She called her lady-in-waiting to her.

"Elmira, I need for you to do something for me. It will be dangerous and require great speed and stealth. I fear entrusting it to anyone else, as

Charlie's life depends upon it, and this requires a little more delicacy and intelligence."

"Anything, milady, anything for you and Charlie."

Rebecca detailed how to get to the portion of the forest that held the mysterious plant, and Elmira left immediately, despite it being the middle of the night. Rebecca settled in, clutching Charlie close to her. She knew it was her last and only hope.

৵৶

Rebecca took a deep breath, slowly let it out, and said, "I heard a funny name the other day. What was it? Oh yes, Rumpelstiltskin. Is that your name?"

The little man's smile dropped, eyes widening at first, then narrowing. "Where did you hear that name?"

"Oh, a little spot in the woods. Perhaps you know it? The best berries grow there."

Words exploded from him, his voice high. "This is impossible! You've cheated!"

"Pray, little imp, how would I have managed that?"

"This I cannot say, but there is no way you could have figured out my name without cheating in some way."

"You like to sing, do you not, Rumpelstiltskin?"

"Stop saying my name!"

"I have a little song for you. Perhaps you'll recognize it.

*'A child's soul
To heal my own,
A name they'll never guess!
Thrice times spoken,
The power to heal,
Without, it means his death!'"*

Here, she paused, gazing at him as he became increasingly agitated. A small smile stole across her lips, the first in quite some time.

"Do you remember what you said after that? No shame if you can't. I'll remind you. 'Never will they guess my name is Rumpelstiltskin. That child is mine!' But you were wrong. This child is mine and will remain so."

Azrael cleared his throat and stood. "We have a deal. We've guessed your name, now help our son."

Instead of words, Rumpelstiltskin began to scream and stomp his feet upon the wooden planks of the floor, moving faster and faster. As they watched in horror, his body fell apart, piece by piece, chunk by chunk, until it all became dust on the floor.

A sudden whirlwind sprang up in the middle of their bedchamber, picking up the fine Rumpelstiltskin dust from the floor and swirling it about. Azrael made to bend over his wife and child, but before he could fully cover them the dust ceased swirling and launched in their direction, covering them in a fine black powder. Aghast, he tried to brush it from his son's face, but the lady stilled his hand and stared intently at Charlie, watching for any change.

When nothing happened after a few minutes, she slumped and held him tight, tears beginning their ticklish path along the line of her nose. Her husband bent back over her, pulling her into his arms, the baby snuggled between them. Her tears fell from the curve of her cheek onto Charlie's face, leaving clean tracks through the black, but neither lord nor lady gave heed.

They missed the sound at first, so great was their desolation. A tiny, smothered inhalation. A quiet whimper.

Then that wee baby stirred, shifted, and let out a weak cry. Rebecca jerked out of Azrael's arms and held Charlie up before her. As she watched, the damage to his once perfect frame began to dissipate, to creep away from his features.

First, the skin mended, lumps diminished then disappeared. Open sores closed themselves, leaving the flesh pink, smooth, and whole. Next, the blackness receded from his fingers, his nose, his perfect baby toes. It was a quick process, and before either had a chance to blink, there lay sweet, whole, flawless baby Charlie, mended.

He began to cry, that familiar, lusty baby cry, telling his mother he was hungry. Warily, she put him to her breast, bruised from his mindless gnawing during the illness. He latched on and nursed.

Rebecca sighed, settling back into her seat. The specter of a decayed gnome of a man would haunt her all her days, but at least they were a family again.

Beside her, Azrael sniffed, swiping his nose across his sleeve.

# MELODY OF BONES
### by Nickie Jamison

Malachi conjured the image of the wealthy Duke's daughter. The small room dimmed as bright blue tendrils of magick arced from his fingertips, enveloping the pan he held above the crackling fire. Flames licked the bottom, hungry tongues of orange lashing along the burnished tin. He thought of the girl with soft honey blonde curls, cherry red lips, and the dulcet tune of her voice as she writhed beneath him.

The water in the pan hissed and sputtered over the rim, splashing onto the hot coals below and sizzling away in a puff of white steam. The sudden jolt from concentration caused the magick to falter. Malachi clenched his jaw, breath hissing through his teeth. He hadn't meant to heat the water so. Boiling bones thinned the fat, made the fat leak out, made the bone hard to grasp. Not good for a flute.

He moved the pan from the fire. The bone inside thunked against the tin. Malachi peered into the pan. The water had turned a light copper shade and smelled of blood and dirt. Through the steamy haze, Malachi saw bits of white ligament, tendrils no thicker than a thread, still clinging to the femur. He pulled the bone from the water and cleaned it with a cloth, rubbing the soft bits of flesh away from the hard surface.

The Duke's daughter flitted back into his consciousness. He thought of the gentle tug of her delicate fingers at the sleeve of his shirt as she pulled him toward the woods bordering the gardens of her father's estate. The moonlight slanted in between the high bows of the trees, and her pale hair danced silver in the dim light.

Malachi set the bone aside. It would need to dry for a few days before he could begin carving his new instrument. Enchanting objects was paltry work compared to stronger magicks, according to the old witch, but she had spent her talents fortune telling for coin. The witch didn't trust Malachi enough to teach him stronger magick, and she'd told him so with her last breath.

Malachi scrubbed his face with his palm. Calloused skin rasped against the three-day stubble on his chin.

Magicks used energy, regardless of a spell's success, and the effort to enchant the flute left him drowsy. He undressed and slid beneath the covers on the straw-filled mattress, the best he could afford on the little bit of coin he gleaned from standing on street corners playing his old wooden flute.

In a few days he would have a new instrument, a better one, made to bring people to him and their money into the tin pan at his feet.

Though he was tired, sleep did not come easy for Malachi. He tossed fitfully, trapped in the void between wakefulness and dreaming. When he did dream, Malachi was a small boy again.

*His back was pressed against the plank wall of the tiny room he shared with his mother above the tavern. Lucien, his mother's John, screamed words Malachi didn't understand. The large man's meaty palm crashed into*

*Malachi's face, and Malachi fell to the floor, sobbing. He looked at the scuffed and worn floorboards. There was a knot in one of the wooden slats shaped like a butterfly, its wings open. Malachi wished he were a butterfly, beautiful and hard to catch.*

*A gurgling noise drew Malachi's attention. Lucien's ham fists were closed around Mother's throat. Her hands beat at the John's angry red face as her beautiful white face became ashen grey. Her lips blossoming into a strange mix of violet and blue. Lucien let go of Mother, and she crumpled to the floor like the sack of coins the other Johns left on the table by the door. Coins she would give Malachi to buy paper for writing his music.*

*The door crashed shut as Lucien left. Mother did not wake up. Malachi tried to rouse her, shaking her, petting her yellow hair, kissing her cheeks, but she slept. She slept with her eyes open, the whites turned pink from crying, making the lovely blue sparkle like sapphires. Mother changed. Her dress was no longer the dingy gray rough-spun, but instead she wore a cerulean ball gown. Her dress was torn at the neck, smeared with muck and blood—just like the Duke's daughter.*

Malachi sat up. He sucked cool night air into his hot lungs and rubbed at his tight chest. The nightmares had returned. He threw back the covers and went to the table. The femur gleamed white in the low light. He turned it in his fist, inspecting. He couldn't wait the few days. He needed to finish his spell now, and the bone seemed dry enough. Malachi summoned his magicks and began to carve.

Malachi's fingers danced along the flute and the party goers swayed to the merry tune he played. The circus dwarf that had long ago taken in the half-starved and beaten orphan boy, Malachi, was much freer with his knowledge than the old witch had ever been. He taught Malachi well. Sometimes Malachi missed the nights sitting 'round the campfire, carving flutes and whistles under the watchful eye of the wizened half man.

The magickal flute garnered Malachi an invitation to the affair. Only just that morning he stood on the corner outside of one of the town's many wine-sinks playing enchanting tunes to the passersby on the street. A Count in a green hat, wide brimmed and decorated with a gaudy purple feather, tossed a worn leather purse into Malachi's polished tin pot. The Count gave Malachi directions to his estate and promised more gold if he played delightful music for an evening.

Malachi accepted the offer and thus he was present, standing in a corner of the grand room, close behind a velvet settee and a few steps away from the table laden with costly wines, ripe fruits, and fine cheeses.

The Duke's daughter stood in the doorway. Melody. He remembered her name. Light shimmered on her golden hair. As she moved across the room, the burgundy folds of her ball gown flowed like cool summer wine. Malachi's gaze was captured by her slender white throat around which she wore a black silk ribbon strung with a cameo pendant. The pendant rested above her bodice in the arc of her breasts. Malachi's breath hitched in his throat, and his tune faded away.

The girl turned toward him, and Malachi's eyes opened wide. He'd been mistaken. Melody could not be here, and the young lady in the merlot colored dress was someone else entirely. She was far more magnificent than Melody had ever been, with soft, heart-shaped lips and skin the color of fresh cream. Her cheeks bore a hint of rouge, in a dewy innocent glow.

Malachi drew his shoulders up and pressing the flute to the curve of his bottom lip, he blew across the embouchure. He felt his magicks licking along the tips of his fingers and drifting out into the room with the notes he played. Malachi could see them hanging in the air, tiny flecks of blue light, some dancing like flames of a candle. No one else could see the glittering orbs gliding through the air and enveloping the beautiful girl in the dark dress except for Malachi. He wanted her, so he played on, weaving the spell to draw her to him.

The girl crossed the room and stopped in front of Malachi, her hands clasped over her heart. Her hands were gorgeous, slim fingers with nails buffed to shine. On the girl's right middle finger she wore a golden ring set with a large ruby.

Malachi looked at her face. Her full lips turned up at the corners into a delighted smile reflecting in the pool of her dark blue eyes. The girl's skirt rustled as she swayed back and forth, caught in the spell of Malachi's flute. Malachi ceased his tune and lowered the instrument. The magicks remained, tendrils of blue light danced in a helix around her.

"You're the musician my father hired this morning? What is your name?" the girl asked.

"My name is Malachi," he said softly.

"Clairette." A flush of pink brightened the rose color on the apple of her cheeks and blossomed along her milk pale throat. She averted her eyes.

"A beautiful name for a beautiful lady."

Clairette looked back to his face, her eyes fringed by long dark lashes. She touched her lips with the tips of her fingers. Malachi watched, fascinated as the edge of her manicured nails skirted the plump curve of her bottom lip.

He resisted the urge to reach out and stroke her cheek, to run a sensuous line across the bottom of her jaw and over her slender throat with his thumb. He wanted to feel her body.

Malachi's mouth went dry. Just over Clairette's bare pale shoulder, standing out in the foyer, was the Duke's daughter. Melody's honey-colored curls fell over her shoulders. She looked at Malachi with a blank expression before turning and becoming lost in the throng of party guests. This was not possible. How was she here?

"Where are you going, Malachi?" Clairette asked as he stepped around her.

Malachi weaved through the crowd, the bone flute clutched tightly in his hand. If she was here, he needed to find her. There. In a cluster of young women, he saw Melody's cerulean ball gown. He reached out and touched her shoulder. When she turned, Malachi apologized. The young woman's hair was too dark, her lips too thin. How could he have ever mistaken that lady for the Duke's daughter?

He turned to retreat when he caught another glimpse of Melody, by the open door that led to the garden. Malachi opened his mouth to call out her name, but a cold pain in the pit of his belly made him stop. One of the guests walked in front of the French doors, and when Malachi could see again, Melody was gone. He had not seen her come inside, so she must be in the garden.

Malachi sidestepped people to reach the garden door. The heels of his shoes clicked against the slate tiles that lined the winding path through the flower beds. A large gazebo stood in the center of the garden, the white paint illuminated by the moonlight. Malachi stepped up into the structure, and the boards creaked with his weight as he turned one way then another, hoping to find where Melody had gone. Crickets chirped, adding rhythm to the sounds of the night.

The path of flowers led into a hedge maze. Melody stood at the entrance. In the moonlight she glowed, her hair shining silver and her gown throwing a ring of light on the ground at her feet. She stepped behind the large swan topiary guarding the maze's entrance.

Malachi stumbled on the step of the gazebo and nearly lost his hard grip on the flute. Gathering himself, he ran into the maze. He was behind her, his heart thudding loudly in his ears as he followed Melody's shimmering gown turn for turn. Right, left, right, right, left, left again, and then right. Just as he would close the gap between them, Melody would slip into another open corridor. He lost track of where he was, following blindly. Unkempt branches grabbed at him from the towering hedge, snaring in his clothing, ripping holes as he swept past. Malachi gripped the flute, and his legs pumped faster. Steps behind her now, he reached out to grab her shoulder, and he narrowly missed as she turned another corner.

Malachi skidded to a stop. His chest heaved as he tried to catch his breath. Melody had turned into a dead end and vanished. The dark foliage of the bush loomed over head, and a few untrimmed leaves at the top shook in the light breeze, mocking him.

She had been right there. He swore it. Malachi spun left then right, but there was no sign of the Duke's daughter. Malachi looked down at his flute, clutched in his fist. The white bone glimmered in the dark. Malachi's jaw tightened, and he breathed in sharply through his nose before setting off for the maze's entrance.

Malachi tried to retrace his steps with little success. He had taken so many turns and found so many dead ends before finding new turns he hadn't seen before that he was convinced the bushes were moving of their own accord. The moon was much higher in the sky when he found an opening that led out. To his disappointment, he had not discovered the front of the maze, but the back and a path leading down into woods behind the Count's estate.

He stood on the edge of the slight slope, looking at the dark tree line below. He decided it would be more prudent to follow the edge of the maze back to the house rather than try to navigate the maze itself and get lost all over again. As he walked, Malachi kept his gaze down on his path, careful not to trip over the large rocks that lay at the base of each bush to keep the dirt from washing down the hill toward the forest during rainstorms.

Malachi walked until he reached a corner of the maze. He turned and in a few paces the sounds of the ongoing ball drifted to him.

"Malachi." The sound of his name made him look up from his feet.

Melody stood in front of him, her hands clasped. Her facial expression was stony and unreadable. Magick blue lights danced in a helix around her.

"Melody, you can't be here. You're dead." His sweet Melody. Malachi dropped the flute and lunged at her. He knocked her to the ground. "No one must know." His fingers wrapped around her slender throat. It was a familiar feeling. Her soft, honey-blonde curls brushed against the back of his hand. Her cherry red lips made the shape of an O, and the dulcet tune of her screams echoed in the air as she writhed beneath him.

Melody's face melted and changed. Malachi gripped Clairette's soft throat and choking gurgling noises came from between her parted lips. With one hand, she slapped at his wrist, and the other reached out into the grass. He tightened his hold on her, watched her lips slowly turn the color of lilacs, and barely noticed the flash of white as she jabbed upward into his throat.

Malachi rolled with the sudden shock of pain and found himself starring at the bright moon and the end of his magick flute. Clairette had speared his throat with the jagged edge. Each breath pushed air through the instrument, and it whistled a discordant song. Malachi's chest and face were soaked in blood. He could feel the pulse of it leaving his body and pooling beneath his head, saturating his hair, and then cooling with the night air. Melody's face floated above him, her lips turned up into a pleased grin.

The music stopped.

# THE GODMOTHER'S BARGAIN
*by Alison McBain*

My mother died so the magic would work. She accidentally killed herself, cutting too deeply into her pulse points and sprinkling too much of her own blood throughout the garden as she tried to summon the spirit. I found her underneath the weeping willows, white as bone, with the blade fallen from her slack hand and standing sentinel over her body.

Although I didn't know what she planned, I dreamed about the spirit she summoned. I did as the dream told me, and I buried my mother's blade deep in the garden underneath the willow trees. I dragged her body up to her chamber and disguised her self-inflicted wounds with paste and blood, creating suppurating sores, before running through the house crying, "Plague!" No one was brave enough to go close to see if I told the truth. Even my father wouldn't check on his *beloved* wife, stopped by fear of the deadly disease.

And I? I was daubed with the same brush as she, cast temporarily down into the servants' quarters in case I disturbed the household with my exposure to my mother's phantom illness. My costly furs and velvets stayed in my rooms. I dressed in brown homespun clothes and slept next to the coals in the fireplace. The servants would not come near me other than when summoned, so the warm hearth was mine alone.

The night of my mother's death, I closed my eyes in exhaustion and fell instantly asleep. I saw my mother dancing underneath the willow trees, her arms and face were frozen in the rictus of death as I had found her, but her legs limber and leaping like a deer. As she spun away, I saw she'd been dancing with a shadow under the weeping trees. The shadow moved toward me in a rush, and I held out my hands—whether to stop it or welcome it, I did not know. I opened my mouth to speak, to scream, to stop it, and later woke on the hearth, my face smudged by the ashes of the fire.

Weeks passed and no one in the household fell ill. I was allowed to return to my old rooms. It wasn't long afterward my father introduced me to my new *mother*.

Her face was round and plump, like a dairy maid's. I had seen her before with my father at odd moments, receiving a stolen kiss in the marketplace, greeting him in a doorway across the square. She moved into the house, along with her two daughters, one of which had my father's eyes, the other his short beak of a nose. It was not long before they were sheltered under my father's name.

"When it happens, do not hesitate," my mother told me the night before she unwittingly took her own life.

I didn't hesitate. When the time was right, I struck, and the old man died.

It was that shrew mistress who suspected me. She was never so easy with my father's sudden death. She tried to keep me as far from her daughters as possible, but it was hard to isolate me without exposing her suspicions. She did her best, keeping me away from the lessons her daughters took, engaging a separate tutor for me. From the outside, one would think she cared.

"How you must mourn your father's death," she said and had my meals sent to my room instead of allowing me at the table. "You need space to grieve in your own way."

In my bedchamber, I ate the food she sent and laughed softly to myself.

It wasn't until after my father's death that everything began to unravel. By then, it was too late to save anyone.

❧

In my sleep, I danced as my mother had danced. When I woke abruptly, the household was silent. Outside the window, the gardens were lit as bright as daylight. It was midnight, and when I stood, my limbs felt as languorous as if I were still sleeping. I moved in a dream down the stairs and through the kitchen, my bare feet making no sound. I stepped over the sleeping servants, the whisper of my fine lawn gown brushing over twitching faces that did not wake.

Out in the garden, the cold ground on the soles of my feet seemed to pierce through the mood. The cold traveled up my calves and into my thighs to lodge in my heart. With the chill, I remembered from my dream what I had to do.

Under the midnight moon, I danced in the garden where my mother had died. From the outside, I was a pale slip of a girl, barely a threat to the deep shadows of the night. Inside, I had my purpose drilled into me from the moment I could walk and talk, the culmination of my mother's life. Underneath my feet, the earth that had drank my mother's blood, that had witnessed her final summoning, shifted and groaned as if from great pressure.

The magic did not work for her, but then again, she was the first sacrifice.

It worked for me.

When I turned in the final circle, I saw a figure resting on a bench beneath the willow trees. The moon didn't penetrate the stark shadows of the drooping branches, so the figure was simply a darker hue against the black. There was something wrong about its outline, something that sucked at what little light might have exposed it, that trapped the moon's gentle glow in a miser's fist and released only more darkness.

"Godmother," I said in jest, and the figure threw back its head and laughed in great and violent joy. I shivered at the sound but didn't dare retreat. "I have a boon to ask you."

"You ask for a gift? But who will pay the price?"

Startled, I replied, "I have already paid."

Laughter came again, but gentler, like a mother's indulgent chuckle. "Oh, child, you understand nothing. You have paid *nothing*."

"Fine." I raised my chin. "What is the price? I will pay it."

The shadow studied me, but I saw it finally nod. "You will." Fingers chopped through the air, cutting the light into pieces. "Give me your hand."

I took a deep breath. Although I had come this far, I did not trust what might happen next, though there did not seem to be many options open to me with such a direct order. I walked forward, keeping my eyes centered on the darker shadows of the willow trees. I held out my hand, palm forward.

A touch, so gentle I might have imagined it and for a second, nothing.

Then a flood poured through me. Behind my closed eyelids, I saw images flickering in quick succession, so bright and fast they made little sense at first. Magic roared through my veins, battered my senses. My mouth was open, an endless scream escaping into the night, but the scream was as soundless as if I had been muzzled.

I found myself flat on my back, staring up at the cold moon. My body felt bruised but filled with a power both dark and thrilling.

"That's the payment? Destroy the king?" I managed to croak in a voice that sounded ancient with knowledge.

A voice rustled from the shadows. "I have given you what you asked. Find my payment, and then return to me. You have a month until I come looking for *you*."

❧

A lifetime marked out in the space of a month. The next morning, my stepmother came across me in the kitchens. She glanced around.

"What are you doing here? Where are the servants?"

"I dismissed them." At her shocked, rounded O of a mouth, I said, "I told them it was you who ordered it and withheld their final wages. No one will take a position with us now. Well, what are you going to do?"

She stared at me for one long moment. Her eyes were dark, her brow furrowed. Without a word, she turned and stormed away.

I stayed in the kitchen. When midday came, I brought up to their rooms a tray of food for my half-sisters, a meal I had lovingly prepared with my own hands. Just as they sat down to eat, my stepmother came rushing into the room and knocked the food to the floor.

In a low voice, she hissed at me, "Try as you might, I will not allow you to do what your wicked heart desires. It is over. You have won."

"Won?" I asked with a smile. "Whatever do you mean?"

"I found what you wanted me to find, the newly turned earth in the garden. Five mounds for the five servants you *dismissed*. We will take ourselves from here, immediately. Girls, pack only the bare essentials. We are going."

My half-sisters cried at the same time.

"Where will we go?"

"Why?"

"It doesn't matter where we go, but go we must. For our lives. For our *souls*." The adulteress hustled the girls past me, making the sign of the cross as she did so.

৵৵

The following day, a knock boomed at the door of my empty house. Dressed in castoff rags left behind by one of the servants, I answered the summons. Smothered in gold braid, a man bowed stiffly to me and unrolled a scroll without pausing to raise his eyes to my unworthy demeanor.

"His Royal Highness, King George, requests the attendance of all the noble ladies of the kingdom for their celebration of Prince Frederick's natal day this evening." The messenger bowed once more, spun on his heel, and strutted off.

I had to wait until the sun disappeared, until the last light left the sky. Whereas poison worked at any time of day, magic—*my* magic—did not. Once darkness covered the earth like a smothering blanket, I pulled the magic into my service, creating from the cursed garden a veritable wealth of accoutrements. From the branches of the weeping willow, I spun a dress that draped around me like sorrow. From the tears cried in the garden by my half-sisters for our father, I fashioned two glass-clear slippers. From a death cap mushroom, I created a gleaming white carriage. Bats descended from the sky, and I transformed them into midnight-black horses that moved in odd, jerking movements, as if trying to take flight.

My arrival at the castle gates did not go unnoticed. Whispers followed me into the palace, followed me as the prince came across the ballroom floor as if entranced and took my hand, while his father, the king, beamed at us from the dais. The prince and I danced all night, long past the setting of the moon. It was not until the air grew moist before dawn, not until I noticed the sky had not quite lightened, that I felt my magic begin to drain away. The sun would kill it completely, but before that happened, there was one more thing to accomplish.

I cast a spell over the crowd like a net. They closed their eyes and turned away for a moment as I walked up to the dais and took the long blade from beneath my skirts—the same blade that had killed my mother I had just dug up from the gardens that night—and I sunk it deep within the breast of the king.

By the time the crowd blinked and turned back to the dais, I was back across the room with the prince. Like the rest, I feigned shock and grief.

After the tedium of the king's funeral and a brief period of mourning, the prince and I were married. But by then, of course, he was king, crowned in a dazzling ceremony that was only outshone by our wedding for its splendor.

After my husband fell asleep on our wedding night, I took the blade back and buried it in my father's garden under the cold light of the moon.

"The price has been paid!" I danced as I had before, following in my mother's footsteps, and the shadows gathered under the willow.

Laughter rang through the garden like a midnight bell, overwhelming me with the coldness of a thousand hating hearts.

"Oh, my little queen, you are wrong. You have failed."

My mouth dropped open in shock. "Failed? But-the king! I killed him. You told me I must destroy the king."

"Yet the king still lives."

"What? That is not the same king! You cannot really expect me to kill everyone with royal blood. Why, even *I* am distantly related."

I saw the task stretching out before me, an impossible and unsolvable problem.

"The king is dead," said the voice, mocking me, fading back into the shadows. "Long live the king."

# LEILA

*by Dan Shaurette*

Her name was Leila, a Romani gypsy by blood. Born under a blue moon, she used to tell me. I met her one day as I was leaving London. I had failed again in my attempts to become a noble's jester. She had her horse cart just off the country road and was seated in front of it, in the mud.

I rode up on my steed, Morning-Star, and asked her, "Good morrow, milady. What fortunes should leave you here?"

"Funny you should ask, sir, as it is usually my job to see problems like this in advance. In hindsight, I suspect I pay more attention to others' fortunes than my own. My horse was struck lame, and I just put her out of her misery, but now find myself with my own share."

"If I may ask, where are you headed?"

"As far away from London, that loathsome town of cheap bastards, as possible!" She spat as she finished.

"Then it seems we are meant to travel the same road and for similar reasons. Those arrogant fools wouldn't know humor if a hyena bit them in the arse. I am sure my steed wouldn't mind the burden of your cart if you would have my company with him."

She blushed. "Good sir, do you believe in fate?"

"I believe in laughter, luck, and love. I suppose my luck could be influenced by fate— perhaps such as our meeting here."

She'd smiled a knowing little smirk I'd come to know well over the years. "Last night, I dreamt of a single star shining in the heavens, one that looked like the white mark on your steed's brow…a morning star."

I was struck speechless, one of few times. I realized then she had the Sight

"Milady, it would please you to know my horse takes to that name."

She smirked again. "Yes, I know…Corey."

I nearly fell off my steed and did so anyway for comic relief. When I picked myself up, I knelt down before her, taking her hand.

"Milady, you have me at a disadvantage. What name has the heavens so wisely bestowed upon you?"

"I am Leila. Not such a remarkable name."

"On the contrary, my dear Leila, its beauty is only exceeded by the lady herself. A beautiful name for a truly remarkable woman. I mean, I don't fall off my horse for just anyone. They usually have to pay me first."

She laughed, and I realized I was falling in love, for I knew it was a heavenly chime only angels before had the pleasure to hear.

I hitched Morning-Star up to her cart, and she shored up the damage caused when her horse could endure no more. A wolf howled in the distance, and I saw in her eyes true fear of someone all too familiar with death.

"We should get back on the road to the nearest village before it gets too dark," she said.

From that moment on, we traveled together over hill and dale, visiting towns and villages, trying to bring some levity into their lives. She would read people's fortunes while I amused the crowd. She became my partner in life and love.

We traveled together for many months. Every new city was exciting for us both. While we didn't stay long in any town we'd visit, we would visit some of them often.

The townsfolk of Norwich enjoyed our shows so much, we considered it home. In the center of the town was a small tavern and inn. Leila always convinced the innkeeper to rent us, cheap or free, a room whenever we stayed there.

One night, after a fine meal at the inn, she took my hand and gave me a gentle kiss.

"Corey, you've made me a very happy woman."

I kissed her, my heart swelling with love. "As you have made me as well. A happy man, that is."

"You've also made me a mother-to-be, and you—"

"A father?"

She nodded, and I kissed her with true joy. After our embrace, there was a small moment of sadness as she wept. I hoped they were tears of joy as she explained.

"I know what you are about to ask, but the Romani never marry outside of our clans, except in the most remarkable of circumstances."

With that, I bent down on one knee before her. "You, my beloved, are remarkable, and I cannot imagine my life without you, no matter the odds. Would you do me the great pleasure of being my bride?"

There was a moment where I thought she may have made her mind against the idea, but then she smiled and said, "Yes!"

With our need now to earn more money for a proper wedding and raise a family, we once again left the town and traveled for a few months. When we had enough, we made our way back to Norwich, where we knew they would love to share the ceremony with us.

On the trip back, while Leila slept, I took a shortcut through a patch of the dark woods. Rumors they were haunted had been told since time immemorial, but I did not fear such superstitions. Leila would have warned me, of course, but she needed her rest, and I wanted to reach the town before nightfall.

It was not ghosts or monsters I should have feared, however. At one small pass, a band of highwaymen attacked us.

"Stand and deliver," the largest robber demanded.

I would have given them anything they asked for had I been given a chance. Without warning, one of them grabbed Leila roughly, stirring her awake with a knife to her throat. Another dragged me from my seat and beat me with his staff. When their comrade tore through our cart and found our money, I hoped they would leave, but things instead got worse.

They scared Morning-Star into running off, with our cart bouncing roughly behind. Two of the highwaymen beat the living glory out of me and stabbed me in my gut. It did not take long before I passed out.

In small bouts of consciousness, I could hear them force themselves on my beloved. I heard her screaming and kicking. I heard them encouraging each other on. When she was no longer sport to their taste, I heard her cries cut short followed by the sickening sound as they slit her throat.

I tried to yell out but could not catch my breath. My eyes, which could not see in the darkness of night, stung with hot tears. In the horrible silence that followed, I passed out. When I woke again, the sun had risen. I pulled myself closer to Leila. When I finally saw the horror of her death, I reached out to hold her, ignoring the pain which tore through me like a red-hot poker.

In my delirium, I thought I heard my beloved's voice.

*Corey...*

At first, I thought she might still be alive, but upon touching her cold, rigid body and seeing her lifeless eyes, I realized it could not be. I heard her again.

*My love for you...sweet Corey...will not die.*

With those words, I passed out again. I looked forward to being with my Leila in Heaven above.

৵৽৶

Liquid fire burned my lips as the droplets trickled down my gullet.

I licked at the searing salty-sweet elixir and found myself craving more. I opened my eyes and was horrified to discover the source was a wrist hovering above my mouth.

"Good, you're awake," said an ancient voice in the darkness. The hunger I felt compelled me to drink. I grabbed the wrist and sucked at it like a teat filled with mother's milk.

"To you, I shall be your new mother. Drink up, but you'll have to stop soon."

I didn't want to stop, and I don't think I could have on my own, such was the need. She eventually pushed me away.

"That's enough for now. Soon I will teach you how to feed on your own."

With those words, I could feel her blood inside me. Changing me. Healing me. Making me thirsty for more.

"Yes, teach me, Mother," I whined.

"Later. Now, we must find shelter before the sun rises. Follow me."

Even in the darkness, I was aware that I could see perfectly. Before me was a woman who could have been only two score years, and yet she seemed to bear the unseen weight of centuries. I looked back in the darkness before dawn at what remained of my beloved Leila.

"I'm sorry, my child. I could not save your gypsy rose. She was dead when I came across your scent, but you were just at the brink. I was only able to save you, my young jester. You have the gift of eternity now to release your laughter unto the world. Fool them, trick them, taunt them, but most importantly, make them all die laughing, my dear."

That was the first of my lessons from Mother. We ran deep into the forest to an area where the trees were so thick and tall no sunlight dared shine down upon us. In there I found

Morning-Star and the cart, amazingly still intact. I walked up to pet Morning-Star, but he reared up at the sight of me.

"Your pretty star-faced one fears you now, but I will teach you how to get close to him again."

She did, and as promised, she also taught me how to hunt with stealth.

Mother gave me warnings about avoiding sunlight and fire, but she told me I could never die. She herself had seen the passing of thousands of seasons.

"I only died once, after drinking from a cursed chalice, but I arose the next night and took revenge by drinking the blood of some of the Roman soldiers who killed my tribesmen."

"Roman soldiers?"

"Yes, I was the dowager queen of the Iceni whose land they stole and enslaved."

I was shocked as she flooded my mind with her memories of war and death. Blood was everywhere.

I didn't say her name, Boudicca, but she nodded a heavy gesture toward me as if I was the first to know the truth of what happened.

"Eventually, I took to these forests to hide away from the horror I had become. I venture out only to feed on the bands of ne'er-do-wells who make the mistake of finding shelter in my woods."

I asked, "Did you kill the ones that attacked Leila and me?"

*Yes, she did, Corey. You should have seen it. Justice was swift.*

"Sorry." I cleared my throat. "What did you say?"

Mother said, "I said, I did, yes. I would have attacked them sooner, but you and your gypsy rose were passing through, and I did not want to harm such a beautiful couple. In avoiding you, I missed the scent of the highwaymen stalking you. I could not deny the aroma of your blood or hers, however, once it was spilled."

The branches rustled and whispered around us. *I am here with you now, my love,* a woman's voice chimed again.

"Pardon?"

"Did you hear that?" Mother asked me. "It's in your blood. It's in the wind." We both paused to listen.

I didn't dare ask because I was not entirely sure I wanted to know the truth, but Mother answered my unspoken question anyway.

"Yes, Corey, that is Leila. Do not be afraid, she knows no pain."

*Only the pain of seeing you alone, beloved.*

A crimson tear rolled down my cheek, and I wiped it away.

Eventually, the time came for me to leave Mother behind, riding solo in the cart with Morning-Star in the reins as loyal to me as ever.

As I rode off, I couldn't help but think of Leila and how empty the cart was without her. In the wind, I heard Leila's voice again. *I will be here with you, always, my love. Even in death, we shall not part.*

# NOTHING TO WORRY ABOUT
*by Charles Frierman*

The people in the small village of Clodswart feared Nothing, but not really enough to immediately be concerned by it. It was just always out there somewhere, but it very rarely made its presence felt in Clodswart. It was rumored that Old Smeltzy had recently been killed by Nothing, but since Old Smeltzy was just a giant golden-haired dog, it was easy for the villagers to put it out of their heads and pretend like Nothing ever happened.

Crazy-tooth Carl, who was Old Smeltzy's owner, couldn't put it out of his head, though. He loved Old Smeltzy with all his heart and just the thought of Nothing being out there haunted his every dream. There was no way he could go on living like this, so he tried to convince everyone else in the village that something must be done.

"I'm sorry, Crazy-tooth Carl. We just can't waste time worrying about Nothing," the town elder said after Carl's impassioned plea for assistance. "We are all terribly sorry about Old Smeltzy. He was sort of a Clodswart mascot in a way, but I'm afraid animals die for different reasons. My dog died of a common cold, and Jed's passed away from an infection following a broken leg. Just because you aren't qualified to specifically say what it was, doesn't mean it was Nothing. I think we all know Nothing is just an old wives' tale."

"You know that's a lie!" Crazy-tooth Carl snapped, his eyes flaring with the pain and rage that only a heart-broken pet owner can exhibit. "Look me in the eyes and say that. Then, and only then, will I believe Nothing is not out there."

*Nothing.*

"That's what I thought," Crazy-tooth Carl said nervously and backed out of the town elder's silent chamber. He had been hoping for, if not help, at least awareness from the town. After his meeting, however, he did not feel better at all and decided to take his warnings to the streets.

"Warning! Warning! Nothing will kill you, just like it killed Old Smeltzy." He shouted at the top of his lungs while ringing an old, giant, rusty bell he borrowed from someone's porch. At first, no one paid him any mind, but soon his message started getting through as more and more people were retreating to the safety of their homes. This encouraged Crazy-tooth Carl as people finally seemed to be getting the message that the world was a dangerous place.

"You can't be here yelling like this. You are scaring people."

"Good!" Carl snapped at the Captain of the Guard, who had snuck up behind him.

"No, it's not good. I need you to run along."

"I won't quit until either everyone is safe or until I stop people from being killed by Nothing. Are you volunteering to help?"

"Look, I've heard about your dog. We all have, and we all feel terrible. We just can't be chasing ghosts or fearing legends. Why don't you just follow me home, and my wife can make you some cider. It will calm you down."

The man seemed honestly sympathetic, which only irritated Crazy-tooth Carl even more. "It's not some fairy tale. It's not a stupid ghost, and I don't like cider!"

"Calm down, Car—" the guard started to say but then there was a scream in the distance.

"Help, help, the Elder is dead!" First came one cry, and then more people started joining in.

"I told you. Nothing is here, and it's real, and it's on my trail. I knew it wouldn't be long. Was Old Smeltzy not enough for you, you sick freak!"

"Stop it, Crazy-tooth Carl. I need to find out what happened, and I can't do it with you shouting and spreading panic."

"I told you what's happening!" he shouted once more. "It's—"

*Nothing.*

There were more screams. Crazy-tooth Carl took his own advice and fled the area toward, what he hoped would be, the safety of his home. Nothing was definitely out there, closing in, and judging from the screams, he was sure the village of Clodswart was finally starting to get the message.

Once home, he walked over to the front of his food pantry and picked up Old Smeltzy's bowl. He kissed it and then made some adjustments to the memorial. When he was satisfied, he put the bowl lovingly back in place.

"I tried, boy, but they wouldn't listen. How can I fight if no one else will help?"

The water bowl did not reply, but a brisk wind did as it blew through the open window almost making a doglike moan. Crazy-tooth Carl stared with a horrified look on his face, then carefully backed away from Old Smeltzy's bowl. Once the wind died back down, he grabbed a couple of peppers from the pantry, being very careful of his old friend's bowl, and retreated over to his couch.

Gnawing on the vegetable seemed to calm him down a bit, and eventually he relaxed enough to close his eyes. He lay on the wooden sofa, let his legs hang over the edge, and for a brief moment all was quiet. Crazy-tooth Carl drifted to sleep and dreamt of Old Smeltzy playing with him by the lake just outside of Clodswart. Carl found himself laughing as the dog ran up behind him and pushed him into the water. When he climbed out, all wet and filled with rage, Old Smeltzy licked his owner's hands, always his hands, and Crazy-tooth Carl could only laugh. Old Smeltzy never had a care in the world, and for the longest time, while they were together, at least, neither did Crazy-tooth Carl.

Nothing could ruin that. Nothing *did* ruin that.

A knock on the door startled Carl, and he jumped off the wooden sofa into an attack stance.

Another knock.

Crazy-tooth Carl ran over to the window and peered out. It was a man he'd never seen before in leather armor, nor did it seem like someone he wanted to talk to now. Something about this guy gave Carl a bad feeling. The man's head turned to the open window, and Crazy-tooth Carl ducked down. It wasn't fast enough, though. He had been spotted.

Another knock. "Open up, Crazy-tooth Carl. I just want to talk to you."

"About what?" was Carl's reply, but he already knew.

"Nothing," the man said somberly.

"Why is it always Nothing, and why is it always me?"

"I'm sorry? I didn't quite hear you too well. Just open the door. Let me in and we can talk about Nothing. Isn't that what you wanted? Someone to listen and help you out?"

The man's words were kind, but they came out sounding harsh and unsympathetic, especially when he continued to pound on the door.

"Did you kill Old Smeltzy?" Carl asked with no conviction.

"I think we both know that isn't the case. Open the door and let's talk about Nothing."

Crazy-tooth Carl opened the door. The man pushed past him, walked into the house, and started looking around. Carl didn't like him and wanted him out, but what could he do besides look on helplessly? The intruder started tapping on the floor and walls, and then moved over to the pantry and rummaged around, accidentally kicking Old Smeltzy's bowl out of the way in the process.

"Who are you?" Crazy-tooth Carl asked.

"My name is Ezjohn," the man said without looking up. "I was the Town Elder's bodyguard."

"Oh? I didn't see you there earlier."

"For which I will forever be accountable, because now he is dead."

"Oh."

The man in leather stopped rummaging momentarily and turned to look at Crazy-tooth a little more closely. "He sent me home because he wanted to talk to you in private because of your dog. You see, the town elder was very sad for your loss and thought it would be easier to console you if I wasn't there."

"Oh."

"You don't sound surprised."

"I tried to warn him that Nothing was there, but he didn't believe me or give help. Now look at him. I don't want to sound mean, but he got what he deserved," Carl muttered, but didn't meet the bodyguard's gaze.

"He got what he deserved?"

"Nothing. I didn't say anything."

"I see."

Ezjohn started tapping on the floor near where Old Smeltzy's bowl had been. Crazy-tooth Carl felt uneasy watching this, because there was a coldness in the man he didn't like.

"Did the captain of the guard have it coming too?" Ezjohn followed up in that same uncaring voice.

"What?"

"I think you know what."

"Fine. Then, yes. He wouldn't listen to me, either. Why won't any of you listen to me?"

Ezjohn didn't seem to be listening and continued to tap on the floor, getting painfully closer. Crazy-tooth Carl couldn't take it anymore and approached. The man either didn't notice him or didn't care.

"I've seen Nothing in action, and it is not something anyone should ever have to see."

"How many times have you seen it in action, Carl?" the man said absently, right as he found a hollow spot covered by a floorboard. He opened it up.

Crazy-tooth Carl didn't answer. Instead, he pulled a hunting knife from a large belt pouch he wore on the backside of his left hip.

"What do we have here?" Ezjohn asked, opening a metal box that had been concealed.

"Nothing." Carl hissed and drove his hunting knife down into the man's shoulder. The strike was a strong one, and it pierced Ezjohn's leather armor enough to injure him, but not kill him. The man rolled away, sprang to his feet, and staggered backward pulling out the knife. The box he had been carrying dropped to the ground and out came Old Smeltzy's remains, along with two human left hands.

"I knew it," the bodyguard muttered.

"You know nothing! My dog was suffering, and no one could help him. The vet said Nothing was wrong, and it was just Old Smeltzy being old. I didn't understand at first, but then I figured it out. Nothing will kill all of us if we let it, so I decided I wouldn't let it."

"Your own dog?"

"Yes, I killed Old Smeltzy. I tried to tell you morons what had happened, but you just gave me sympathy and pity. You didn't heed my warning, nor did you care, so I knew I had to take action. Can't you see, if Nothing started feasting on our town like it tried to do to my dog, we'd never get it out of here. That's why I killed the Town Elder and that other fellow. I saved them from Nothing, just like I will save this whole town."

The guard once again lunged out of the way as Crazy-tooth Carl dove at him. This time he was able to counter by tackling the wild man to the floor. Crazy-tooth was completely berserk, and his adrenaline was pushing him to levels of strength he hadn't experienced in years.

"Get off me now or die." Ezjohn struggled to say, but he was barely holding his own. Carl then lunged in once more and bit the man's face with his crazy-tooth. Ezjohn used Carl's momentum against him, rolled him over, and rammed the knife into the wild man's heart. Ezjohn crawled away, but when he looked back, he knew there was no longer a threat in the room.

"Beware, Nothing is coming." Carl grunted, holding on to life as long as he could.

"You are nothing, Carl, and without you, we have nothing to worry about."

Ezjohn pulled the crazy-tooth out of his cheek and discarded it on to the floor.

# THE CURSED CHILD
*by C.S. Kane*

The young woman clutched a jagged dagger in her small hand. The blade was speckled with copper-colored rust. As she stood at the window, she moved to and fro like a fragile twig of willow swaying in the rough breeze. She drew a breath and with a grimace, paced along the creaking floorboards of the cluttered cottage. The wood-wormed, hollowed-out slats beneath her bare feet groaned, threatening to give way. She glanced to the dark alcove in the corner where a plump baby lay in a tattered crib. The child gurgled and giggled within its blackened, straw-lined manger. Every so often, the woman stopped pacing, turned, and with anxious fervor, stared out of the small, latticed window. She surveyed the sharp horizon streaking across the black moors.

"By all the stars, where is she?" she muttered.

She tucked her raven hair behind her ear and stalked across the room. Her tattered skirts swayed about her slender body as she padded by a heavy oak table. She allowed her fingertips to press against the dusty bottles and yellow tinged folios covering every inch of the splintered surface. She strained her eyes as she studied the manuscripts. Thick beeswax candles flickered, throwing misshapen shadows all around the small room. Something caught her eye. The needle from her crooked spinning wheel glinted in the candle light. She wrapped her long arms around herself, moved to the alcove, and leaned her heart-shaped, freckled face over the crib. She stared upon the child. Her brow furrowed.

"A full moon encircled in red and lo' it is such a frightful night for such a beautiful babe," she whispered. She ran her thumb along the blade, keeping her gaze firmly upon the child. "You have been cursed since the day you were born, and now the blood moon has risen. The bones have spoken to me of your fate."

The embers of the fire crackled as the last licks of flame from the pungent turf faded. She shivered. A thunderous bang resounded around the cottage as the door thudded open. The maiden swept in front of the crib, coiling her body like a snake. She raised her blade. Her jet black eyes narrowed, and her mouth twisted in a snarl.

"Clontara, wait, please. It is only me, Agatha," she protested as she raised her frail hands, displaying her empty, wrinkled palms.

Clontara dropped the blade to her side.

"I thought it was them. I thought they were coming for her."

Agatha frowned. "They are." She kicked the door closed and hobbled to the table.

Clontara strode across the room and stared out of the window. A number of luminous green lights appeared in the distance. She counted twelve.

"It is all of them, then." She smacked her lips as her mouth went bone dry.

"Yes, and he follows them playing his song." Agatha sidled to the cradle and scooped up the baby. "The word on the wind is they will do it tonight."

"They will not have her."

"They want her flesh for feasting and her blood for sacrifice to him."

Clontara glanced out at the lights and back to the baby.

"She has my blood as well as his, and I will not let them have her. She has so much to do. She is the only one who has the strength to defeat him."

"Their magic is so strong and dark." The old woman shook her head.

"I am her mother. I will be strong for her. I will save her."

Clontara grasped her long, black hair in one hand and twisted it. With the other she raised the blade and hacked as close to her scalp as she could manage. Her long raven hair released from her head, and she dropped the knife to the ground.

"What are you doing?" Agatha asked. Her toothless mouth opened in a silent gasp as she clutched the baby. Her thin lips peeled back and caved in over her dark, wet gums, aghast at Clontara's actions.

"I'm doing all I can."

Clontara ran to the spinning wheel and settled upon the stool. With nimble fingers she wound her hair upon the golden flax and began to pedal. Her bare foot tapped rhythmically as the strands entwined, twisting and tangling around each other in a strong bond. With the thread, she wove a short yet thick, square, black shawl.

"I hate to tell you, but that will not shield the child's skin from the hexes of those witches." Agatha paused. "They will be upon us soon. They are marching steady to the sound of their drums.

Those drum skins are made from the skins from their enemies. You know this, Clontara."

"Yes, I know full well how cruel they are."

"You must know then that shortly the sound of his whistle, the whistle whittled from the backbone of his own mother, will ring out across the blackened moor. I beg you to listen. You must run, Clontara. You must run now!"

The sound of the coven's snare drums rattled through the cottage window with a rat-tat-tat.

Clontara looked up, her eyes wide with burning intensity. "The coven will find me in the woods. They are my kin after all. The woods are where my sisters and I were born." She paused. "In the swamp."

She whipped the blanket and rubbed her fingers over the soft hair. The shawl of black seemed to shine with the interwoven flax.

"It is beautiful," Agatha said.

"Give her to me," Clontara said. She lifted her arms, took the child from the trembling old woman, and smiled. Her face was soft and kind as she wrapped the infant's plump body inside.

"What are you doing?"

"The babe must be bound in black and..." She handed the child back to the old woman.

"And?"

"She must be bound in black and blessed with blood." Clontara snatched up the knife and dragged it across the pale skin of her forearm. With a grimace, she took the child once more and cradled her in a tight embrace. As she held her bleeding flesh over the child's head, she whispered,

*"Blessed with blood in a mother's love, bound in black to hide your tracks."*

"Clontara, they are almost at the door."

"You must save her now. Go on. Take the crib. It is made from thick reeds that I seeped in tar. Put her in it and run. I have seen it in the scrying stones and the bones I cast. If you get her to the river, then she will live."

"If I don't?"

Clontara stared down at the child and frowned. "Go out the back now. Go on! Do you hear me?" She snapped her head up. "She must live or the world will be plunged into darkness—his darkness—for eternity. Everything good will die by his hand."

Agatha nodded, her mouth agog, as the child was thrust back into her arms. Clontara grasped the old woman by the shoulders.

"You must run down the hillside and into the woods. Get her to the river. Do you understand me, Agatha?"

"I...ah...yes. I understand."

A loud series of thuds reverberated around the cottage.

"They are at the door. Go," Clontara whispered. She watched as Agatha moved quietly out of the cottage.

The thuds were repeated.

"Time to face them," Clontara said.

The candles danced in leaps before going out in an instantaneous puff of smoke. She stood frozen in the darkness, her eyes darting around the room. Outside the gaggle whispered and laughed.

"Oh sister... Sister, come out and see your kin."

A chorus of cackles rang out.

"We must see you tonight. Come forth and greet us with some family hospitality."

Clontara stood as straight as she could, feeling the warmth of her own blood as it ran in a thick, sticky stream down her arm. She raised her head and stepped with a slow and steady pace to the door. She reached out to grasp the cold iron ring.

"Do not make us come in there for you, sister. We would hate to have to drag you out by your glistening locks," a shrill voice stated.

Another outburst of raucous laughter followed.

Clontara drew a sharp breath and flung the door open. As she stepped outside into the lime green light emanating from their crooked staffs, the sound of shocked gasps filled the air. She smiled and raised her head higher.

"What has she done?" one of them whispered. "Look at her. Look at the state of her."

"She has hacked at her very own head," another sniped. "Her bones protrude from her skin like one that has been starved."

"Yes, yes. Exile has not agreed with her it seems."

"She should never have left the bosom of her master. Wasting away she is."

"What do you want, sisters? I have no time for your irksome games," Clontara said.

"Oh-ho, she stands so regal for one dressed so poorly," a short, plump witch laughed.

"She is but a wretch of a witch, an embarrassment to our kind."

The shrieks of amusement rang out around the moors.

"Enough." The eldest and tallest of the group stepped forward.

Clontara eyed her closely as the hooded crone circled her.

"She reeks of blood, sisters."

"I thought you loved that smell, Gregantia," Clontara whispered.

Gregantia wrapped her bony fingers around Clontara's still bleeding arm and dipped the crystal tip of her staff deep into the open wound. Clontara winced and inhaled with a sharp breath.

"She has cloaked the child in some way." Gregantia raised her staff and analyzed the blood-soaked crystal. "She has conducted a blood blessing."

"You will not find her," Clontara said.

Gregantia sneered, her mouth twisting into a crooked, toothy grin.

"Sisters join me," she snapped.

The witches formed a semi-circle enclosing Clontara, her back pressed against the cold stone of the cottage.

"No," Clontara said. She shook her head from side-to-side. "No!"

The witches raised their gilded staffs and directed the luminous lime-green staff-lights toward their sister. Clontara's bare feet rose from the muddy ground. She could feel a raging heat behind her as the thatch on the cottage burst into flames. Her arms rose as her tensed body was hauled up into the night air. The light from the cottage blaze illuminated the crooked faces of her persecutors. She stared down upon them, unwilling to believe the blood-thirsty crones shared her blood.

"You brought this on yourself," Gregantia snarled.

Clontara's limbs twisted in jagged, angry thrusts. Bones burst from beneath her delicate skin. Her blood flowed from the puncture wounds. Clontara screamed as her body broke and crumpled in violent jerks. She looked deep into Gregantia's eyes. They seemed to burn as fiercely as the violent flames behind her.

"You will not have her," she screeched. Her voice cracked as blood erupted from her throat in a savage gurgle.

"Ha! You fool. Before you die you need to know our master hunts. He hunts in the woods. He shall have his sacrifice." Gregantia flicked her staff upwards and howled with glee as Clontara was flung back into the roaring flames consuming her humble home.

❦

Agatha's feet burned as she pelted through the thicket. Her creaking, ancient joints had not moved as fast for many years. Her temples burned as the blood pounded around her ricket-bent body. The child was silent, and for that she was grateful. Agatha stopped dead. Something was up ahead. She could hear rustling and grunting. She narrowed her eyes. They were strained in the darkness of the night. She gasped as she made out a dark, hunched figure nearby. Clouds of rancid breath burst from its long-snouted face. She could smell him and his rot—the scent of blood and death. Her eyes widened as she saw the horns. He was as gruesome as she had heard in the old tales and fireside stories.

Wheeling sideways, Agatha ran as fast as she could. Glancing back, she realized he had caught her scent. The sound of twigs and branches snapping behind her forced her onward. She darted behind a wide, old oak tree and held her breath. For a moment he stopped, sniffing the air. She looked from the corner of her eye as he passed. Taking her chance, she went back, retracing her steps. She knew she had to camouflage her own scent.

Agatha leapt over and under the twisted roots of the trees. She heard his hooves pounding after her once more. She did not dare to think about the nature of the beast that followed her. Agatha understood what Clontara wanted her to do. She knew Clontara had been the scrying sister. If this was the plan, then all she had to do was play her part, and the child would be saved. She exhaled as she ran down the gully bog leading to the river. She pushed her old legs into it, immersing herself in the thick, slick dirt in a bid to sheath the smell of her skin. It rolled over her body as she pushed onward, holding the cradle aloft. She reached the river bed and slid the basket into the water beyond the reeds. It was invisible in the blackness. Only she knew the child blessed with blood and wrapped in black was floating away from the evil that wanted to consume it.

She turned, treading softly back into the woods, the muck dripping from her hunched frame. She wiped her face and looked around the silhouettes of the twisted, spine-like tree trunks of the forest. It was his breath on her neck that alerted her to his location.

"Where?" the demon grunted.

Agatha turned and studied him with her slate grey stare. She grinned a gummy grin, and her eyes danced.

"Where is she?" The snarls came faster.

"Gone. You shall not have her, demon." She guffawed, raising her bony fingers to her gaping mouth. "Just as her mother planned."

"Don't speak to me of that wretch. She is unworthy."

"Clontara is a queen," Agatha retorted.

"Ha!" a voice echoed behind them.

"Gregantia." A low growl echoed around the woods.

"Clontara is nothing. Clontara is dead," Gregantia boomed as her coven swept behind her. "Such power, such a waste."

Agatha's shoulders slumped.

"Where?" The demon craned its neck, cocked its grotesque head, and barred its sharp brown-stained teeth.

Agatha shifted from one foot to the other. She looked around the pale, hungry faces of the sisters and back to the rabid demon. His nostrils flared, his lips peeled back to expose a frothy foam of dirty saliva dripping from his wide, snapping mouth.

"I told you. The child is gone. It is foretold you will see her again. She will return, and all of you will die. The child was cursed by each and every one of you, but she was cradled in her mother's love, a love more powerful than the hate you spew." She drew a breath. "A love that saw the ultimate sacrifice made." She smiled and stood up as straight as she could. "The cursed child will return and claim her vengeance against you, demon."

Agatha laughed aloud as the witches fell upon her. She smiled safe in the knowledge those who wanted to feed upon the small, innocent child were doomed to dine on the bones of a tough old woman. As the sound of her own snapping limbs filled the night air, she closed her eyes and succumbed for she knew under the blood moon that the child was simply a shadow being swept to safety and away from the corrupt clutches of the wicked demon and the twisted sisters of the coven.

ॐ

The slate grey sea swept toward the jagged rocks of the fast approaching coast. The waves broke in flashes of shocking white across the bow of the wide oak ship. Long slats of rain thrashed over the billowing, crimson sails. A girl stood tall at the helm of the vessel, steering it through the storm. Her face was set sternly against the pelting squall, and her long hair whipped around her with the ferocity of the rough wind. Her eyes narrowed as she scanned the ragged coastline of her destination—her birthplace. It was lined with charred trunks of evergreen trees long since turned black. The island looked rough and desolate. There would be no scavenging gulls circling the coast. There was nothing worth picking at. As the ship drew closer, the girl made out smoldering stacks on the hills.

A tall, stout man moved to her side, and she glanced to him. "What are they?" She nodded toward the smoking piles.

"Possibly beacons for incoming ships."

"Who else would come here? The place is rotten to the core with violent deeds of the demon and his crones. We have heard as much from those below decks."

"Please be careful believing all you hear, Captain. It becomes hard to decipher fact from fiction in times like this."

"Those who managed to escape his clutches and now sail with us have explained their experiences in full." She shook her head. "Who are you to doubt them, Hala?"

"I try to take everything with a pinch of salt. I am a seafarer after all."

"I'm one of them remember? When you saw me in the sea you understood the desperation my mother must've felt as she put me on a course to the open water. When you plucked me from it, you didn't have one shred of doubt my story was one of sorrow. You gave me a name and loved me as your own. No questions asked."

"That I did, little Owa."

"Their reports must be taken as they are given. This is a place where insidious evil breeds, and our companions fled in abject terror."

"Now they all return with you—for you."

"No, they have come for themselves. They want to reclaim their home. They remember it better than I and have seen first-hand what these monsters have done to it. I can only remember flashes. The smell of blood, some chanted words, and then the cold night. After that, only the sound of water and then your kindness. I am forever grateful for you."

"No need for thanks."

"Now, this is not a place for traders to visit. Those stacks cannot be beacons."

"True. I'm not sure what they are then, Captain. They could be for some sinister purpose. Sacrifice perhaps? Who knows exactly what they do here? As you say, the reports suggest their depravity knows no bounds. The inhabitants of that island have danced to the demon's tune for so long, who knows what we may find?"

"Drop the anchor and assemble the crew. We must make our approach. Dawn breaks."

She watched Hala go below deck. He had been loyal to her since he had scooped her up from her tar-lined basket and wiped the blood from her face. She owed him her life. He returned with a clatter of people in tow. They emerged from below, some with hands raised to their eyes and others blinking, into the morning sun. Men and women from the plundered villages, exiled mountain elves, fae from the burned down forests, griffins from the south coast of the island, and many more creatures. They stared up at her. She whistled to Hala and bid him to take hold of the ship's wheel.

"My dear country folk, we are almost upon the island. Most of you ran from here. This was your home as it was mine, and they stole it from us. Their evil has seeped into the soil and corrupted the woodlands. The rivers have been tainted by the innocent blood of our families and the air polluted by the smoke of burned villages. We shall avenge those who have been taken by this wretched coven and its master."

"Their magic is strong. How do we fight against it?"

"Witches are creatures of the night. They soar in the shadows. We are arriving at dawn for a reason. They'll be at rest. We will sneak upon them and dispatch as many as we can while they sleep. I will not pretend we will all survive. This will be a difficult battle, but it is ours, and we must win. This demon's horde has displaced you, murdered your families, and ravaged your land. We have to win."

"What about the demon?"

"I will take care of the demon. I am my mother's daughter." She glanced toward Hala.

He nodded.

She raised both her arms and opened her fists to display her palms. She murmured and in each hand a ball of swirling flame burst into life. Gasps swept around the ship.

"She *is* a witch like her mother."

"Yes, I am." Owa dusted her hands together, dissipating the charge between them. Her fingers fell to the hilt of her sword. "Many of you knew of her. You have told me the stories, and I can only hope to live up to her name. You all came here freely, and this is just a small demonstration of my power. Believe me when I say I have as much to lose as you. We fight together. What say you? Are you ready to reclaim our lands—our lives?"

One by one they unsheathed their daggers, swords, and axes and held them aloft. The feathered creatures opened their wings wide and cawed. The hooved stamped their feet. The charge of energy that rippled through the ragtag crew was palpable.

"We shall lower the narrowboats now my friends. We must enter through the river mouth." She smiled and held her own sword aloft. "Death to the demon!"

The narrowboats moved by stealth up the river. They watched the banks closely for any sign of life. The paddles became slick with sludge as they came to the gully bogs. With a finger pressed tight onto her lips, Owa signaled for them to follow. Crouched and clustered tight together they moved through the scorched remains of the trees and came upon a weeded verge leading to the open fields. Upon the blackened plain, mounds of heaped rags were scattered.

"Look, Captain, they move," Hala whispered.

Owa stared at the piles and noted the rhythmic movement.

"No, Hala, they breathe. It is the coven, and it seems they have converted more to their damned legion. We must charge upon them on my signal."

"What of the demon?"

"I do not see him. I do not know this terrain. I am, however, drawn to that structure on top of the hill. Do you know what it is?"

"I don't."

"Bring me Janaro, the Elder Fae."

Janaro swept beside them in an instant. Her translucent wings fluttering lightly as she hovered by Owa's cheek.

"You need me?"

"Yes, Janaro. You are the one here with the most knowledge of this place. Tell me what that derelict edifice is?"

"That, my child, is the remains of your mother's house. That was where you were born and where she died. No, forgive me. That was where they murdered her."

"Do you believe the demon could be in there?"

"Where else does a tyrant live other than above his subjects? They lie in the valley plains, and he could be atop the hill. Yes, that seems to be a sensible conclusion."

"Thank you. Go back and spread the word that we charge on my signal."

Owa gripped the hilt of her sword, raised her free hand, and stood. As she took her first step toward the field of forsaken witches, she felt the crowd behind move with her. They pounded the earth, churning up mud. Yells of unrestrained anger filled the skies as their blades sliced into the mounds. The remaining members of the coven jerked from their slumber at the sound of their kin being slaughtered. They jumped to their feet, eyes wide with surprise. Cloaks were flung back, and they raised their bony hands with talons clawed into positions for casting. The screeching began.

Bright balls of burning charges flew through the air.

Owa ducked and dived, slicing as she went. She could hear the screams of her companions as they fell under the blistering bolts of magic the witches lobbed. She turned to see a griffin ripping at the throat of an enchantress. She watched an ally elf torn limb from limb by two old crones. Her head pounded as she pushed through the carnage.

Ahead she saw a sorceress clutching a tall staff with a green light beaming from it. The woman screamed orders at her sisters. Owa ran at her. Their eyes locked. The witch raised her staff and pointed it. The stream was strong and fierce. Owa raised her arms and crossed them, casting a sphere of protection around herself. It was too late.

Upon seeing the head witch cast the stream, Hala leapt into the path of the dark magic. The blast hit him in the chest burning a hole through his torso. He fell to the ground.

"Hala!" Owa screamed. She dropped her arms, releasing the protection spell and ran to him. His eyes were lifeless. She looked up at the witch and snarled. "Why are you doing this? Why?"

"My dear child, why don't you come and give your kin a sweet embrace?"

"You—you're Gregantia—you killed my mother!" Owa yelled.

"I did, and now I'll kill you." Gregantia flicked her staff, and Owa's sword was stricken away from her grip. It hovered, suspended in the air. With a crackle it melted into a smoking metallic pool like a piece of tin in the blacksmith's furnace. "Now you die."

Gregantia clasped her staff in both hands and raised it above her head. Owa braced her stance and in her open palms created a charged ball of light between her fingers. She shut her eyes and felt the pulsating power she was creating. Every piece of anger was pushed into the luminous orb. Gregantia made her move, blasting a stream toward her niece. Owa retaliated, pitching her cast toward the oncoming curse. A loud explosion burst through the air with the impact. Gregantia's charge was deflected entirely by Owa's. The ancient sorceress gasped as the power of both spells bounced back upon her. She raised her arms to no avail as the double hex stripped her skin away. Her bitter bones dropped to the sodden ground in a pile of smoke.

"The demon," Janaro whispered in Owa's ear. "Kill the demon and win this war."

Owa sprinted up the hill and entered the ruined remains of her mother's cottage. She kicked through the rubble and burned oak beams. Something caught her eye—a skull, well-aged and charred lay in the mess. She picked it up.

"Mother."

A piece of metal glinted in the spot where the skull had been lying. A small rusted dagger stained with old blood. Owa studied it, her eyes wet as she realized it too belonged to her mother. She slipped it into her belt.

"Where are you, demon?"

Owa scanned the structure of the cottage and noted a hole in the floor in a soot blackened alcove. She sidled to the gaping opening and peered down. Torches lined a hollowed out tunnel, the descending path stretching deep down into the earth.

"I have you now," she whispered. She stepped gingerly into the confined space.

The tunnel finally gave way into an open, round chamber. Torchlight danced across the wide dirty floor. In the center of the room was an elevated seat of bones upon which the demon sat, wearing a demented grin.

"Finally," he snarled.

"You have been waiting on me?"

"Yes. This is foretold."

"You are set to kill me?"

"I am set to eat your heart."

The demon lunged from the throne, clawing his way across the room, the ground smashing under the weight of his hooves. Shots of orange-hued flame burst from Owa's open palms as she ran around the outside of the space. The demon tore after her, snapping his teeth with wild abandon as the hexes glanced of his thick, spiked, leather-like back. She cut into the center of the chamber.

"Damn you!" Owa screamed as she scrambled to the top and clambered onto the throne. Her hands throbbed as the magic bursting from them began to fade to nothing more than crimson ether.

"You wane. Not strong enough." The demon laughed and stalked toward the plinth. "You are mine."

He smashed at the throne with his thick forearm, sending the bones scattering across the floor. Owa's legs jolted as the structure toppled downward. She yelled as she landed with a hard thud. Rolling onto her back, she gasped for breath. The beast leered over her, its breath reeking as it studied her face.

"You were always cursed." It leaned back a little, baring its teeth for her to see. "Fool."

"You are the fool." Owa whispered, lifting her head from the floor.

The demon paused and glared down at her. Owa felt for the small dagger in her belt. Her fingertips gripped the blade.

"What did you say?"

"You are the fool. You see, the curse you gave me became my cause."

Owa swung her arm out in a wide forceful arc. The small blade sliced through the fat neck of the beast. His eyes widened in shock and horror as dark emerald blood spilled from his throat. Owa rolled to the side and hoisted herself from the dirt. She watched as he fell, clutching at the wound. The squealing stopped, and the pained glint in his eyes diminished. He lay still as stone and as dead as the curse.

# THE HEALER'S GIFT
*by Lynn McSweeney*

She woke, just before dawn, bone-weary and vexed in equal measure, to a loud insistent Rap! Rap! Rap! at her cottage's heavy oak door. The carved sign hanging above it proclaimed her art. All agreed she had the healer's gift. They were thankful when sick, resentful when not, leery always. None of the village would idly seek her out, here at the edge of wild woods, in pitch black, far from their own homes, so Airmid supposed whoever-it-was must be in the middle of an actual crisis. The night had been full of such. A wee babe gasping for breath, its mother frantic, had proved to be whooping cough. The farmer who hauled a rough turnip cart bearing a long youth in fits, eyes rolled back white, had feared his son possessed. She had finally persuaded him that Saint Dymphna herself had suffered the falling sickness as a blessing, and could be called on for protection.

So once again, she scuttled out of bed as quickly as she could, and propped herself up with the ash-branch crutch she still must use two full months after her ankle had broken. The Jarl's borrowed horse had thrown her on yet another pre-dawn mission of mercy. Miserable beast. The horse, and she herself now. No rest for the wicked.

Her animals, too, had roistered for hours: chickens squawking midnight alarums; Bastian yowling mournfully, then abruptly vanishing (no doubt to hunt mice); deaf, white-muzzled Bran banished to the barn for his howling. Now dog and hens were at it again, heralding this new caller. Her slow-to-heal bones told her the night remained as damp and chill as it had begun, that first cold, ground-blanketing fog that presaged winter.

The knocking grew more rapid. She hobbled to the door, her only light the banked embers at the hearth. Quashing both pain and temper with a quick blessing ("godhelpyou...if you're drunk!"), she shook the rough linen work-gown she'd passed out in, a vain attempt to smooth it. She flicked the leather strap that covered her spy-hole and peered at the stranger on her stoop. Though she was respected, even feared, a woman alone couldn't be too careful. She hoped a healer's reputation protected her.

The persistent knocker looked to be but a lad, perhaps twelve, with a face milk-pale under wild dark hair shooting off in all directions beneath a loose hood. His light, clear eyes eerily seemed to find her own, though she knew he could not see her through the door, in the dark. She did not recognize him from the village. For no reason she could name, she shuddered.

"Who are you, and on what business?" she barked through the door, reluctant to open it. Her churlishness amazed her. To a child in need!

The boy's eyes widened. His voice was gentle. He was so very white.

"Good mother, I am footsore and frozen, and hungry, and thirsty. I have travelled far. Your sign said Apothecary. Let me in from the cold, warm myself. Give me sustenance or I sicken. I have coin to pay you." His accent might be Danish.

At his first words, the mad ululations from the barn quelled. Frantic hens lulled.

Her hand started for the latch, then stopped short. A moth of a thought flew in. A child alone, wandering this befogged night. Well-spoken, bearing coin, literate. Never the full story. Gazing at him eye to eye, she took some small comfort that neither of his were hidden by the cloak covering his head. She stepped back from the peephole.

"A moment," said Airmid.

His voice rose in a wail. "Good mother! I beg you, let me in. Dawn comes…" He broke off.

Ah, dawn! She pondered. Shouldn't a cold boy welcome dawn? Though with such thick fog a-ground, sun's warmth would be slow to break through. He had already asked entry in the name of the Good Mother twice. If he asked a third time, she'd have to take him in, be it unlucky or not. If he was one of the Good Folk, 'twere better to be generous right off. Ah, well, seeing he had both his eyes, she could at least be sure he wasn't the Wanderer in disguise. Though He too would be welcome.

She took her cane and drew a circle around her person, dragging it slowly with all her weight on it, so it never left the floor. She then scored the length of her threshold in the same manner. She gave thanks her daughter, Grainne, stayed with Beccyl, Airmid's own sister, so she risked but her own safety.

"If…" she cried, opening the door upon a small, shivering figure, shining swan-white in the pearling grey fog, like chalk-cliffs by moonlight, approached by sea. He stared at her wild-eyed, like some desperate creature of the woods caught in trapper's snare.

"If?" he repeated, hope in his tone. So, he knew the bargaining way—she'd guessed right. He was an old soul, young-faced.

"The way is barred, unless—you swear to harm no living soul that draws breath in this dwelling, whether coming or going." The words sang through her. She hoped they covered all.

"I do so swear!" He leapt across the threshold as she drew the heavy door wide. He danced to the right, avoiding the circle she had traced around herself, and ducked back swiftly from the quickening light of the open door. This dawn would have no pink to it.

"Good mother, close it!" he commanded.

She did so, glancing at him sharply. His eyes had narrowed, giving him an older look.

"Ask no further in the Mother's name," she chided him. "I'm pledged to tend you. Sit." She jerked her chin at the hearth, the very back of the house, far from door or window. He nodded, and scrambled to the stool standing before it.

As she stirred the embers with the poker, adding squares of peat, she looked him over. He returned the favor. By the ever-increasing firelight and barely-there dawn light, she beheld eyes the color of cool grey pebbles, hair dark as midnight. A sodden travelling cloak the color of peat hung limply over black woolen hose and boots. Quality stuff. His hands and face seemed bloodless. His cool eyes nonetheless burned her. She put on the kettle.

"What are you…needing?" She would not ask "wanting." Tales held the trooping folk had strange desires. Nor did she ask his name, reluctant as she was to part with hers.

He stood and bowed, a proper little adult. "I am called Weald Walker."

She almost snorted. More of a description than a name. Which could mean merely that he travelled forest and land, and this she already knew, as obvious. A cautious child, then.

"I require warmth. An egg or two if you have them. Drink—whiskey. Likewise, if you have it. And some corner by the fire to sleep undisturbed, full this day." He crumpled back onto the stool, as if dizzy.

"You may call me Mistress Healer," she replied, no more forthcoming than he. Beneath linens kept in a large wooden chest, she unearthed a large sheepskin and an old tunic that had belonged to her long-vanished man. She exchanged them for his soaking wet cloak and set that upon a hook by the fire.

She took a jug down from the cupboard where she kept her herbs, and poured a mugful, handing it to the boy. He grasped the mug, inhaled its fumes, but did not drink.

He glanced from the edge of his eye at the door, and squinted at the thin line of faint grey light growing by degrees on the threshold. He held himself carefully, as if poised to jump.

"Are you Heaven's prisoner?" Her question quiet.

"None but the sun's." His voice was a child's; his words those of a man. He held her gaze. "And…yours?"

"A guest can never be prisoner." She'd made that bargain when she allowed him inside. She quoted from memory.

> *"Who jails another*
> *Becomes prisoner's prisoner.*
> *This my vision, for*
> *When one brother is barred,*
> *Another then must be his guard;*
> *Time spent as ward lost,*
> *Same time both men's cost.*
> *And though both may at last go free*
> *Never that time again will be."*

"It was my father had the book-lore. Scholars let him copy texts," she said. "He showed me the scroll once–writing all tangled like the worst ivy. He told of a great king who wrote poetry in a land far from here, long ago."

"It sounds like a riddle." His mouth broke into a small smile, like a weak sunrise. "I hope it's a promise."

"My mother was Healer before me. She'd knowledge of herbs, bone-mending, the moon's influence, the sun's journey—and she honored guests. Her path is my own."

And she prayed he would remember whose guest *he* was when darkness fell again. She did not think she'd enjoy being his prisoner, either. Her mother's larder had also included stories of visitors. Host could quickly become hostage.

Airmid limped to the door. The stripling with lordly manners flinched as she made to open it.

"Eggs," she said. "You'll explain your ailment to me when I return with them." She cracked the door only as much as needed to hop past it. All at once Bastian surfaced at her heels, and bolted out the door ahead of her, a ginger streak. The mist swirled about her thinly, a-shine with the faint light that told of sun's rise near.

Clumsy on her cane, it took her a good quarter hour to arm herself with a basket, fetch four eggs, settle her suddenly squabbling-once-more hens, and shoo them to their penned yard. Morning broke, fretfully, through fog, the sun a dull penny seen through tattered cloth.

When she carefully wedged open the door again, Master Weald lay in a faint before the fire, naked beneath the sheepskin, glowing like the moon. He seemed longer than he had when he'd been standing, his limbs and chest more like a youth's. As she reconsidered his years—fourteen?—she gentled the basket down and scurried over to him. Kneeling awkwardly, she placed one hand upon his sweat-beaded brow, expecting fever, but he was cold as the stone flags he lay on. She placed both arms around him, hoping she could lift him on but one knee. With his eyes still closed, one marble arm shot out to grip fast her shoulder. His clutch was steely as a blacksmith's. Airmid emitted a gasp of pain and fright. His eyes flew open and found hers, with no recognition.

"It's me. I'm the healer." She willed him to know her. Memory returned to his gaze, but his clasp never loosened. He pulled her down to him and covered his body with hers.

"Warm me," he ordered, teeth chattering, a rhythm like the clatter of spoons against leg beating time to a jig.

She tried to pull away, but found she was prisoned in his shivering arms. Through her cloak and gown, she felt winter seep into her, slowly chill her blood. He was far, far colder than the damp air without, and however he'd managed that, without her body's heat he surely risked frostbite. She stopped struggling then, and embraced him close as babe to breast, growing ever colder even as he basked and warmed at their press. She shuddered in small convulsions atop his icy body, freezing before the fire, all warmth drained from her.

The clasp on her shoulders slowly relaxed. "Enough, Mistress Healer. Your blood has warmed me." He rose, blanketing himself in the sheepskin, and offered his hand to her. He pulled her up in one vigorous, deft motion, holding her steady until her spasms passed. She at last got her cane under control, and put her full weight on it, standing up. He was, she saw with no surprise, taller than she, just. He sank onto the stool.

"Eggs" he whispered.

"First, clothe yourself." She grabbed the worn, soft tunic Dagbjørn had never come back for and though trembling, tossed it one-handed to her visitor. He shrugged into it, indifferent to his nakedness while he swapped fleece for linen. He was long all over, fair as a swan, save for black thatch. The tunic fell below his knees.

She bent to retrieve the strawful of eggs and reached for the skillet hanging by the fire. Frying was fastest. Might warm her.

"No!" he insisted. "As they are."

He then took an egg and placed its small end between his eyeteeth, which were very sharp and long, making him look fox-like. The upper fang pierced the shell neatly. He sucked up its contents within seconds, opening wide his mouth to reveal the red, glistening yolk. Each egg he ate in this manner was bloody as the first. Fertile eggs. From hens with no cockerel.

How on green earth was that even possible, with no male around for her lady-hens? The old braggart who had long lent his loud crowing to announce each daybreak had been dead these past two weeks. And a very tough and stringy stew he'd made. Though she'd never yet slaughtered a one of her creatures, she would not waste one's remains.

Weald took the shells and pitched them into the fire, where they burned with a gold flame.

"Luck ever follows me," he said, as if explaining the question he sensed in her.

His tongue pinked out and deliberately licked clean the last red sheen from his mouth. He yawned, his gaping maw a cavern lined with knives. "I must rest. Let no sun touch me." His bright grey eyes glittered like glass. "Where?"

She looked up, considering her daughter's spot. Grainne usually slept in the loft atop a ladder, where warmest–but also brightest. Airmid's own sleeping arrangement—a bunk in a cupboard—

was darkest. He would no doubt prefer the dark to the warmth. She pointed the cane at her own nook. Dragging the sheepskin along, he flung himself into her bedding, twisting round and round, coiling himself down and deeper into the nest of straw, feathers, fleece and quilted counterpane, reminding her of a dog or a fox. When content, he pulled shut the cabinet doors. She closed the curtain that quartered off her sleeping corner, additional precaution against light.

As her guest seemed to have settled for the day, she drew open the cloth at her window upon a clear, cold morning. The nearly-leafless limbs of trees, the dried berries left on the bush, all were limned starkly in the pale light, no trace now of fog. Wishing she'd done so much earlier, she fingered a braided square of straw that hung over her door, four tied ends spiraling off from its center. She found the kettle, poured tea, splashed an unwonted jigger of whiskey into it, and drew her good leg up under her onto the settle, where she puzzled this dawning day's meaning. She ate something to break her fast and soak up the whiskey, but could not recall its flavor. Only it wasn't eggs.

The morning fretted away. A few townspeople came by at intervals, for remedying. She greeted each in a half-daze, double-checking each dosage, but sending them away quickly, pleading exhaustion and her cane. Cold, cold she was still.

For the first lenitive, she decanted a cordial of cherry, a parchment of willow bark, and a few grains of poppy into a soothing concoction. This was Old Evan, whose weak lungs had long ago succumbed to the smoke of turf-fires, the sting of cold winters, and who had not much time left on earth. He was escorted by his no-longer-young-herself daughter Nuala, already a grandmother, she of the sharp gaze and mean mouth. Though Nuala delved about the cottage with her glowering squint, she somehow failed to note the fine boots and cloak at the fireplace, nor did she ask about the drawn curtain behind the kitchen. Not a breath of sound stirred from her bed snug, neither snores nor tossing-and-turning. It was as if no soul lodged within.

Old Evan promised the healer an extravagant ten large jars of hard cider in the coming weeks.

"Though Young Bevan has taken over the scatting, and I let him layer the pomace a' by hisself, I'll 'low our cider's good as 'tever was!" he declared between coughs. "I learned my lad all my secrets, all my secrets." He winked at her.

She smiled agreement to his generosity, knowing Nuala would never honor the quantity. She'd count on a jug or two, less than poppy cost.

"You'll need to take whiskey with this as well, for it to have its full effect." Airmid had made this decision on a whim. Let him feel no pain. And let Nuala leave a little coin at the distiller's. She grinned a cat's grin back at Nuala's curdled glare at her.

Some hours later, Airmid bundled together a posy that included tansy, more willow, pennyroyal, and some sweet herbs, along with a prayer, to be taken as a tea by a skinny, chattering, quick-breeding rabbit of a lass. Tammy's "flow" problems might well be just one child-catching too many. Not yet nineteen, four children hatched already. She pressed the importance of the ritual's timing on her, the tea to be taken with the prayer to Blessed Brigid, by the moon that shone in her cycle's middle. She told her to come back each month for the same.

Tammy babbled at her, gave her a vague promise of a joint of venison:

"Do my Randal hap run down a hart."

Just as vaguely, Airmid brushed aside talk of barter. That young brood would need all such hoped-for meat they might come by, were they to hale out the winter. She also was wary of benefitting from poaching. Her bonds with the Jarl were close, and she wished never to chance losing his protection.

"Nay, Tammy. P'raps your Randy might help me come Spring, dig up a few young sweetbrier I've marked by the river. I'd need his help planting them nearby." She thought the spot by the old well would do. "Has he a cart?"

Brier rose had many uses. Their autumn hips could remedy bleeding gums and mend bones. Ah, the joy she'd always found roaming the wildwood to visit their loamy beds! Such pleasure might well be less next year, and each year after, given her ankle, its future troubles. Too well she knew how bones once broken never mended in full.

Tammy nodded. Her freckled cheeks stretched in a grin. "Sure I'll make him do the same for our own then! I do love the way they smell. Randy courted me with roses." She reddened.

"And when they are grown your sons will cut wood for me when my bones are old and my daughter far and the winter hard." As Airmid spoke of years yet to come, she felt the weight of them already, but Tammy gasped, taking it as some sort of prophecy. She'd need to watch her words with this one.

Planning for next week, next spring, next year, as if they were a bard's epic, bound to unfold in story. Cider; roses; cordwood. *What if I'm not here tomorrow? That boy is danger, could be my doom. But he had sworn.*

All the day she'd kept track of the sun's arc through its journey, as if a lodestone was dragging and scraping along the inside of her skull in the same direction as that yellow orb in its blue dome. She had long felt the tug of the moon, her blood and body telling full from new. But feeling the sun in the same way was a new skill, one she did not treasure. She ventured out once around mid-day, blood pounding, shoulders scrunched, the top of her head feeling the strong pull of a magnet, lined up right atop her spine. Its scalding light narrowed her eyes to slits, like her cat's, and made them water. And still she felt chilled, even beneath its warm rays.

She scattered corn to pecking beaks, flurried wings, competitive squawks, hoping for no more eggs from them. In truth, she'd begrudge her visitor more. Wanted no more red-yolk miracles.

No sign of russet-tailed Bastian or yapping Bran in barn or garden.

Then scuttling fast as she was able, glancing down at the earth against the glare above, she made the scant shade of a mountain ash at woods' edge, close to the tumbled old stones of a hut long ruins. The rowanberries were still plentiful and black. She broke off a living branch with an apology to whatever soul was buried nearby, and as thanks left a small loaf made with precious honey. Then scurried back to the house, eyes blinking in relief as they adjusted back to the gloom.

As afternoon waned, she sat before the fire with a small knife. She neglected entirely the potatoes and cabbage she usually prepared at this hour. As though still befogged in dream, she hazily whittled crude, curling chips from one end of the rowan branch. Once she'd put tea to the boil, she held the branch briefly to the flames, just enough to char and harden its carved point.

A thin wind began its whistle. The beams above her creaked in harmony, the rhythm conjuring up lines of the verses she'd recited to her guest earlier, memory of her father's voice rolling in awkward cadence, uneasy in translation of a tongue long dead. The wind seemed to sing the last stanza, the one she had not uttered aloud.

> *Who claims a prisoner, meets four roads:*
> *To grant kin's ransom: corn, kine, gold;*
> *To heed captive's plea—kingly free him;*
> *Or sleep fox-eyed to let a fox flee.*
> *But if these high roads be foresworn,*
> *The just road take by morn:*
> *Than two be prisoner, better one dead.*
> *Then grant him honor high as a king's,*
> *And show this mercy: take his head.*

The afternoon shaded to early evening, sun low in the horizon. The wind picked up, branches whipping the stone flanks of her cottage, badgering its thatched roof. Over its wild thrashing she barely heard the faint knocks at her door heralding the arrival of her third caller, a reed-thin, ragged, red-haired woman, panting heavily, in labor. Not much belly to see on her.

She led the woman to the settle, sliding out an extra panel to make a narrow bed. "The babe comes before its time?" Airmid asked softly. The red-head nodded grimly.

Guessing she was a Traveler by her coloring and her dress, Airmid asked no more questions, but began boiling water and laying out rags. She massaged the woman's back, introduced herself, and learned the woman's name, Aven. She wondered if Aven's people had abandoned her by some roadside hedge, to deliver her baby alone, catch up if she could? Airmid had heard rumors of this, thinking it but ill-will spread about tinkers. But by Aven's gaps in the telling, she gathered this child was no tinker's, nor fathered by husband. She had slipped her people when she'd first felt the one within her quicken.

"And when…?" asked Airmid. A month ago. So the child was likely three months early. Mother of Mercy.

The next hours sped by in a blur of staunching the blood that was leaking from her charge, pouring a tisane of herbs down her throat (mostly for luck; as of scant help, or not enough), and giving her a hand to squeeze when the contractions came. Aven continued to bleed.

Airmid saw there was little hope, gave her tincture of poppy, felt with her hands for the trouble. The cord was coming first, wrapped around a very small head.

This was beyond any skill she had or herbs she knew of. The gods had decreed the outcome. Her spirit wept within her, but she showed Aven no tears, though doubting she'd notice.

A loud crash rang out from the bed chamber. Cabinet doors banged open. She looked up from her patient, saw the curtain swing back. Her eyes darted to the window. Twilight had fallen, the sky purple, a thin moon showing. Trees danced to a high wind's tune. When she glanced behind her again it was with a start. Weald had arisen.

His eyes hawked on the laboring woman. They seemed a paler grey now, glittered like ice. His nostrils flared in and out, breathing in time to Aven's heaving. His cheekbones were arched, his brow more pronounced, he had a strong chin. Ropy with new-found muscles, no baby fat left to him. The tunic just covered his thighs.

He suddenly loomed by her side, quick as a blink. Staring. His red tongue darted out.

Aven struggled to speak, her time upon her. "If… the baby…call it…" Then she cried out what might have been a name, either her god's or her lover's, the long yell her last breath. The clenched hand slacked, loosed its cage of fingers that had kept Airmid's prisoner. Her chest stopped heaving, rose no more. She would help nothing further in ushering her own child into this realm; she'd passed on to another.

Airmid steeled her will, armed further with a prayer, and drew forth a tiny blue form, strangled with its cord, no bigger than her hand. She quickly unwrapped the cord, started to tie it off. Ghost of a chance, but she was bound she'd take it. She took a deep breath, put her mouth to its nose. Felt her wrists grabbed, her head shoved back. Weald clasped the un-breathing figure to his chest, leapt to the stool, brought the bloody cord to his mouth.

"No! No!" she wailed, springing for them, but his lips peeled back in snarl, and he swatted her away. She fell against the table, losing her crutch. The buffeting storm's cries became a high keening, drowned out her own.

Weald bit into the cord and drank until it turned white, then pinched it close. His head swiveled like an owl's to the neck of the grey doll he cradled, piercing it swiftly with his eyeteeth, just as he had the egg. His eyes shone like stars in the night sky, remote and cold. His mouth gleamed wetly.

Wobbling on her feet, Airmid found the rowan branch and stabbed at his chest with it. He took no mind of her, only shot one hand out and kept her at arm's-length until he finished. He then finally looked up, stared at the rowan branch dangling from the hole in his tunic, puzzled, then gave a short laugh. The little thing in his arms was pale and clean now.

He let go Airmid's arm, strode to the dead woman, and placed the dead child at her breast.

Airmid sat down quickly at the end of the settle. Her ears rang and her head spun. She gawped at Weald. He gazed back. Rain sputtered down, first a scattered hissing like spitting fire, then suddenly a rushing stream. A spear of blue flashed behind her eyes. Its hammer cracked rock not two breaths after. Suddenly her tears overflowed, anger and sorrow mixed.

"You didn't even let me slap the babe, see if it would cry! Breathe! Live!" she shouted.

His steel-blue eyes met hers, a great calm in them. His lips were now clean. "I swore to you, to harm no living soul that draws breath in this dwelling, whether coming or going."

Gentle his next question. "Would the babe have lived out the day? Even if you'd given it breath? No."

"But why not the mother? Nor was she breathing!"

"She was already dead," he said, as if that was explanation. He shrugged. "Luck ever follows me."

"Call–THAT–luck?" she cried.

Weald pointed to the tinker woman. "Well, she was unlucky, but she might have died in a ditch just as well." His tongue flickered against sharp teeth for one last taste. "Lucky for me—and the town—that she came here—to us."

She was silent, chilled to the bone as she considered his implications. Her Grainne stayed last night in the village.

He bowed to her as he had that morning and chanted.

*Blood wasted*
*Is gift refused.*
*Gift refused*
*Is giver scorned.*

*Second blessings*
*Seldom come*
*To wastrels.*

"That is my own translation," he told her.

She saw pity for her anger in his eyes, as if he guessed that all who crossed her threshold became kin to her. And that would include he himself. Tears still ran in a stream down her cheeks, but slowly dwindled to a trickle, then a glisten, then but a faint shine. He retrieved his garb and boots from the hearth, dressed quickly. He came close, towering over her, and she noticed the shadow of beard at his chin. He opened his purse, held out a gold coin.

She shook her head in refusal.

"I want no gain for this night's work. Go! Never again darken my…"

"Say not never!" His countermand issued forth in a low, deep growl. Her words were silenced in her throat.

He closed his fist around the coin. "We may meet yet betimes." His manner lordly again. "Bid me farewell only, and swear no oaths, lest you e'er have need of me. I would not have you foresworn, when time comes that help is mine to give."

He turned and pulled his cloak, wrapped the unfortunate mother and child within it.

"No fear, they'll be treated with all honor according to the custom of my people," he said, answering the question she dared not ask.

"And what manner of people are they?" She risked her voice again.

"Not. Travelers." His timbre was low and solemn, yet tinged with a merry edge, as if he told a joke to himself.

*Perhaps they are a host...* She did not finish even the thought.

He opened the door and started out on its step, the bundle in his cloak seeming to weigh nothing. The night was cold and clear; the storm had swept by, its fury spent quickly as drunkards' fisticuffs. He turned to her and spoke, his gaze far away or inward.

"I owe a healer's gift. Perhaps several." He smiled then, showing his large wolf teeth. "It is lucky to have me in your debt...Airmid."

Ah, he must have caught her name when she'd first given it to Aven, even though the sun had yet been in the sky; he could hear when sleeping, then. She found she was not pleased for him to have it.

He seemed to know it, and gave her his parting gift. "In your tongue, my name would...perhaps...be..." He thought a bit. "Summer's Bane. I am ever Winter's child. If ever you find you've need of me, I will come to that name called."

She knew that was the closest she would get to his real name. She would think of him as Summer's Bane whenever she dreamed about this night in years to come. He had never really been Weald.

He took long strides as he bore away from her, a strong young man perhaps in his twentieth year, the woman and child in his arms buried under his cape, as if weighed down by no burden at all.

She stared into the clear dark after he disappeared for a long while, wishing, hoping, to see him never again. But heeding his caution, she refrained from praying for it. She wondered whether she would even recognize him if they were to meet years hence. Would he be older than she? or younger once more? And if they (when they) met again, would he have by then fulfilled the promise of his youth, become a well-wrought man? She shuddered, to think she might prefer him so. What gift he might then demand, or give. Oh, let them never meet again!

She latched the door against the evening and its phantoms. Hobbling on her cane, she glanced at it in disgust, then suddenly threw it down. She took a tentative step, then two, then three. Her ankle held her weight without complaint. She could not tell how long the drudgery of cleaning up took her, but she managed it with the old deftness she had once taken for granted.

She aimed for sleep. First tea and whiskey. She noticed a coin gleaming bright on the table. *Ah, he hates debt as much as I. But how we do love obligation.*

She turned in for the night, hoping for the first rest in days. Her coverlets held no smell either of him, nor, thankfully, of blood. Once abed, her ankle never once sung to her of agony, and no dreams plagued her.

She woke, just before noon, refreshed and easy in equal measure, to a cousinly Rappity! Rap! at her cottage door. The day was bright and warm for the season. She looked down at the thump! of

Bastian landing on all fours from his perch overhead on kitchen's beam.

Her caller from the village was Beccyl's bondsman, a scrawny, stunted, smiling man, bearing a pail.

"Aonghas." She nodded to him.

"Your sister sends fresh milk." He carried it in for her. Bran followed him, tail wagging, grey snout filthy, eyes awash in apology. "She heard from Nuala you weren't looking well at all yesterday." He looked her up and down. "But in truth you seem to be all in all recovered. Why, you look as fresh as a maiden—you seem to have lost your years!" His appraisal became guarded. "Watch now, or we'll all be thinking there's witchcraft afoot!" He gave an uneasy laugh, trying to make of it a joke.

"Ah, now, Aonghas," she reassured him. "The healer who sells remedies for a living needs prove their merit." He thought it over with furrowed brow, then nodded wisely in agreement. Bastian slinked around her ankles, urging breakfast. A saucerful of that creamy stuff.

"Pray tell my sister I'll stop over next day; we'll toast the New Year. First of November—I'll treat you both to Old Evan's cider!" She hoisted the pail, decanting the white flood into a jug.

And she never picked up the ash-crutch again.

# BRIAR

*by K.L. Wallis*

"What the hell are you even doing, man?" Looking at the map and exhaling, he raked his fingers through his hair. The entire trip had been a disaster. He had been nothing but lost since he arrived in Germany, but then that happens. It doesn't matter where you are when your life is upended. "They said, 'Everyone speaks English. You'll love it!' They said. 'It'll be good for you.' Ha!"

No. Being alone in a foreign country after just having his heart ripped out only served to make him feel more alone. What *was* he thinking? Not only was he lost, but he had no one to turn to as he did in the past. He looked to his satchel on the passenger seat and imagined her sitting there with her feet up on the dash—even though he'd tell her a thousand times not to—as she followed the map with her index finger and scolded him for missing the turn off to the left. In the end, she was the one who had turned away, taking the kids, his pride and joy. He clenched his hands into fists so tight his fingernails dug into his palms. He missed them so much it hurt.

He fumbled for the door handle, seeking fresh air. Stepping from the matchbox car, he fished around in his satchel for his cigarettes. Lifting one to his lips he lit it, relishing the familiar sound of flint on steel followed by the small, brief flicker of flame. He hadn't smoked in years, because she didn't like it. *What the heck does it matter now?* Inhaling deeply, he absorbed the beauty of the woodland. *So, this is the magical Black Forest? Not much black about it, really.*

The warmth of the sun as it shone through the thick twist of boughs and leaves left dappled patterns on his face. A swift gust of wind rustled leaves around him as he exhaled a plume of smoke. On the breeze, he thought he heard the forest's harsh whisper, "See me."

A chill shot up his spine, and he involuntarily shuddered. He pondered whether to turn back in hope of finding at least a hint of civilization before nightfall. He didn't like his chances. He stubbed out his cigarette and folded himself back into the car, gunning the tiny engine as he turned back toward town.

A way up the road, he noticed a faded For Sale sign, but there was not so much as a hint of any property so deep in the woods, none he'd seen anyway. Curiosity got the better of him, and he pulled over. Upon closer inspection, he saw the trace of a narrow path winding ahead beside the sign. The breeze blew, and he swore it hissed, "Yes."

Ignoring the gnawing in his gut to get back in the car, he slung his satchel over his shoulder and started along the path. *Why not? I came here seeking adventure.*

In many places he had to step over obstacles which had grown over the forest floor or duck under low slung branches. Thankfully he wasn't arachnophobic like his sister. She wouldn't cope with the copious cobwebs he encountered deeper along the way. As he moved further along, the path became so overgrown the sun struggled to slither through to the floor. *Now the forest is living up to her name.* The trail ahead was strangled with thorny vines he had to break to get through. He snapped most of them with his hands, but some were simply too thick. As if willing him forth, the tangle eased itself apart, shaping narrow crevices which he could struggle through.

It was late afternoon by the time he emerged from the thicket. *Great. Looks like I'll be sleeping in the tin box tonight.*

As the wind picked up, a voice like sawdust hissed, "See me."

His hat flew from his head as a litter of leaves swirled around his feet. He turned his back on the sunset and saw the spires of a tower piercing through the lofty tree tops. "Yessss."

Despite the itching of his consciousness, he ignored his better judgment and trudged back into the forest in the direction of the spire. He idly pondered how for the price of a unit back home he could probably buy the place. *King of my own castle. Ha! That'll teach her for shacking up with some other bloke.* The thought filled him with a sense of purpose, drowning out the voice in the back of his head telling him to turn back.

He reached the grounds of a neglected courtyard just before sunset. A beautiful stone arch framed the terrace, surrounded by thickets of wild roses. Two big wooden doors with elaborate wrought iron *fleur de lis* encasing them towered over him, and he cautiously stepped forward over lichen-covered cobblestones. Looking up he saw that on all sides, vines snaked their way up and around the dark tower walls. The windows were beautiful stained glass, but he couldn't be sure what story they depicted. They were murky, red, and difficult to see through. He positioned himself to heave open the heavy wooden door, but to his surprise, it yawned open as of its own accord.

Inside, it was pitch black, despite the splice of afternoon sun provided by the open door. A chill came over him once again as he stepped foot into the darkness.

Instinctively, he called out, "Hello?" He was met only by the sound of his own echo. He shuffled around his pocket for his lighter and flicked for a flame. The hollow blackness swallowed up the tiny light. He stumbled as his toe kicked at something on the floor. The flame went out, leaving him in almost complete darkness.

He cursed. "Bugger me!" The air felt as cool as the morgue he worked in. He didn't know whether it was the chill or the inky blackness which made the hairs of his arms stand on end as he fumbled again for the comfort of his lighter. *Flick, flick.* Nothing. His heart raced as he desperately willed the flame to appear. *Flick.*

"C'mon…please…" *Flick. Flick.*

Flame sprang forth, providing a small, warming glow. "Yes!" The hot flicker singed the tip of his thumb. The house creaked and yawned in response. He dismissed the sound. *Creepy friggin' house.* With his tiny etch of light, he bent to peer at the thing he had tripped over. It appeared to be a mannequin. The child-sized dummy sat cross-legged on the stone floor in front of what appeared to be a stuffed Yorkie terrier. The dog was frozen mid-prance, its front paws suspended off the ground. *How did it stay in that position without falling over?* As he straightened, so did the hairs on the back of his neck.

He was suddenly aware of a presence behind him. He spun, but saw nothing in the dark, not even shadows. He carefully traced his steps back to the door and found it shut. His breath caught in his chest. *Who closed it?* It wouldn't budge as he strained to pry it open. He tried to calm himself. *Old doors will jam…There has to be another way out.*

He reached for the wall with his free hand and side-stepped along it, fumbling for a more substantial source of light. His hand found a panel of glass set into the wall. He rubbed at it with the sleeve of his sweater, clearing away a thick film of dust. The last rays of sun shone in through the window, providing a narrow beam of dim light. He breathed a little easier, taking comfort in the outside world. He turned back to the room and saw shapes in the shadows.

Curiously, not one of them fell within the gleam of light, but before him was a room of human figures. Mannequins, no doubt, like the child and toy dog. They were all dressed in old-style clothing from the medieval times or thereabouts, he guessed. They stood too deep in the dark to make them out exactly. Minutes later, his newly found light was rendered useless as the sun dipped behind the mountains. He reached for the shape of a sconce on the wall. The flame from his lighter obediently appeared when he flicked it, but it was dim and threatened to extinguish as he touched it to the bracket. He released a breath he didn't realize he'd been holding, as the torch flared with flame.

Many eyes shone in the light, making him feel as if they were all fixed on him. In the scope of illumination of his new light source, he saw many mannequins frozen mid-step. Some looked at each other as if engaged in conversation, while others seemed to be dancing in pairs. Some even held goblets. He peered into one of the dull silver cups and saw that they contained a dark substance. *Wine? At least whoever owned this place was thorough in their creepy re-enactment.*

He lit the brackets around the room, and, slowly, the scene was unveiled from its black sheath. Curiosity overcame his sense of fear as he touched one of the figures and marveled at how lifelike they were, as their skin dimpled at his touch. Fascinated, he weaved his way through the maze of dummies, toward an archway which led to the scene of a grand feast.

An unknown king and queen were seated at the head of the long table. Knights in dust covered armor stood menacingly over them with great halberds in their silver-plated hands. The grand assortment of food at the table caused his stomach to rumble. He hadn't eaten since breakfast.

Knowing better, he plucked a shiny, deep red apple from a crest of colored fruits. He sheepishly tested it, scraping it with his fingernail. *Most likely wax.* One lush bite revealed that it wasn't. Sweet juices filled his mouth as he saw the skeleton of a turkey on an otherwise empty platter. It appeared to be intact and therefore, had to be decomposed, yet there was no smell...except for the musky stench of neglect the entire building exuded. Slightly unnerved, he backed out of the room. *Why would they have real food?*

As he turned around, he came nose to nose with a mannequin in the doorway. *What the…he wasn't there before. The doorway was clear, wasn't it?* The mannequin's eyes bore into his. Not daring to turn his back on the thing, he cautiously slunk around it. His stomach knotted as the building seemed to roar.

*Just the wind. It's only the wind.* He clutched his torch, fearing the darker corners of the room. Some of the other figures appeared to have shifted slightly, but he couldn't be sure. *Creepy freaking house!* All he wanted was to get back out. *Into what? The eerie woods?*

He laughed. He was reasoning with himself the way he reasoned with his children back home when they freaked out during the summer storms.

"They can't hurt you," he said aloud. Satisfied it was, in fact, all in his head, he gathered the courage to explore further. A sense of longing washed over him, willing him onward as he stood at the base of a grand staircase. It was as if something were calling to him. He glanced back at the room of frozen figures as he proceeded onward, touching his torch to another on the wall as he passed it by. As he wandered down a richly carpeted corridor, all the doors to the rooms along the way were closed. He tested one, but it would not open. There were no mannequins here. A door at the end of the corridor stood ajar, inviting him in.

He apprehensively pushed it all the way open, revealing the base of a stone staircase. It didn't seem as dark in the stairwell as the moonlight crept in through an embrasure cut into the tower above. A sense of anticipation drew him forth. Several hundred steps later, his legs throbbed. He stopped to rest and catch his breath. Peering out through a narrow slit in the wall, he saw nothing except the sprawling waves of black treetops, their leaves glossy under the light of the full moon. An owl hooted somewhere nearby. As he recovered, the tower groaned. Obediently, he started on upward. The moonlight cascaded down upon him as he reached the landing at the top of the stairwell.

"Finally!" He could see the sky through a gaping hole in the pitched roof. Lighting the sconce mounted by the doorway, he spied a great canopied bed on the far side of the room. Stepping over broken tiles, he advanced to check it out. Sleep invited him. Only, when he drew close, he saw the beautiful young woman lying on top of the covers, her hands crossed over her chest. *Another mannequin?* Her chest rose and fell as she drew breath.

He set down his satchel and extinguished the torch he carried. He didn't need it anymore in the moon-bathed room. He sat beside her, entranced by her beauty. He knew the tale. It was his daughter's favorite, but he didn't believe in fairytales.

He shook her in an attempt to wake her, but she continued to sleep ever soundly. She was deathly cold. As he moved to cover her over with his sweater, he noticed she was dressed in the same fashion as the others. At least…most of them. The man he backed into—was he dressed differently? *Stop it. You're tired.*

His eyes fell on the lovely maiden once more. *True love's first kiss…but I don't love her. I don't know her.* Still, he caressed her face tenderly, touching her lips. They parted slightly at his touch. His heart fluttered at the small reaction. He bent closer to her, unable to resist her sweet perfume. The softness of her lips against his melted away the lingering shreds of fear from his earlier encounters. She stirred in his arms, pulling him closer to her, kissing him back with passion.

He yelped as her teeth bit his lower lip. He tasted his own blood. When he pulled away, he was met by scarlet eyes. Her crimson teeth glinted in the light of the moon. He stood, but she snatched out and grabbed his hand.

The sound of music drifted into the room from the direction of the stairwell. Bewildered, he dared not anger her as she wrapped her arms around his neck and began to sway. He was as a mouse in the maw of the cat. *She wants to dance?*

He heard the faint sound of a dog barking as her lips touched his throat. Images of the faces he had seen in the ballroom flooded his mind as her dreadful animal teeth pierced his flesh. He winced at the sudden pain and went rigid in her arms. This was it. There was no point in struggling. He was hers. He was always hers. His heart raced as she viciously sucked the life from him.

That man…yes, he was wearing a tracksuit…the child a school uniform…the dog a collar…

Wanderers like him, forever ensnared by the lovely Briar Rose.

# CURSE OF THE ELVES
*by Sara E. Lundberg*

Jenna frowned as her husband, Frank, shook his head. No, they would not have enough money to pay the rent—again. It was their last warning. Eviction would follow. They would lose not only the butcher shop, but their apartment above, as well.

What was a poor couple in the midst of a recession supposed to do?

What she did not expect him to do was to give away a still good—well, maybe not good, maybe more like questionable but still sellable—hunk of cured meat to one of the homeless guys begging out behind the shop.

"Goddamn it, Frank. We could have at least used that to feed ourselves. What are we supposed to eat for dinner?"

Frank sighed. "It's better this way. I ate some of that same batch for lunch yesterday, and it gave me the runs."

They took stock of their empty larder and went to bed with only a cup of ramen between them.

"We'll have to close up shop tomorrow," Frank said as they drifted off to sleep.

Jenna bit back bitter tears. This is not what she had in mind when she'd left her first husband for Frank four years ago.

The next morning, Jenna awoke to the wondrous smell of baking. She smiled for a moment, but the moment shattered when she realized Frank still snored next to her. She jolted upright.

"Frank, wake up. What is that smell? Is the house on fire?"

They blundered down the stairs, and much to their amazement, there were two dozen neat little meat pies lined up on their counter, and a line of people stood at the front door.

They both blinked questioningly at each other. Where had the food come from?

She reached out for one, stomach grumbling.

"Jenna," Frank warned.

She was too damn hungry to care. She bit into one, and the hot juices flowed over her tongue. Perfection. She moaned in appreciation of the delectable treat.

"This might just save the business!" Jenna threw an apron on over her night clothes and yanked her hair into a ponytail.

"Are you sure this is a good idea, Jenna? If you didn't make these, and neither did I, where did they come from?"

Jenna rolled her eyes. She didn't care if fairies magically made the pies for them or if the homeless guy out back decided to pay them back for their kindness. They were going to make a killing.

She flung open the doors, and people pushed their way in.

"We smelled this amazing smell from blocks away, so we had find out where it was coming from," one woman said.

Another man bought two for himself, and two more to go after he had eaten the first two. "I have to share these with my co-workers. They'll love them. Beats a fast food breakfast sandwich to death."

The comments and the customers kept coming until they were down to their last two pies. Frank finally grew a pair and ventured to eat one of the pies himself. His eyes grew wide as he chewed.

"That might just be the most amazing thing I've ever put in my mouth," he said.

She gave him a naughty look.

"You know what I mean." He rolled his eyes. "Split the last one with me?"

She nodded, but just as they were about to cut it in half, Frank looked up and saw the Hoffman twins standing with their faces pressed against the glass. It was common knowledge their folks were in worse straights than even Jenna and Frank.

Jenna sighed and nodded to her husband's pleading look.

He grinned and took the last pie to the two boys. Their eyes lit up, and they devoured the thing mercilessly. They ran off after that, happily sucking the juices off their fingers.

While Frank cleaned up, Jenna tallied the morning sales and breathed a heavy sigh of relief.

"We can make the rent, even some of the back rent, and we have just enough to pay the vendors for our next shipment." She frowned. "Only problem is, we won't get it until Tuesday next week. Not sure what we do until then."

Frank just smiled. "Someone is watching over us. We'll be fine."

She rolled her eyes. *Whatever.* She was pretty sure it was a one-time thing. Asking for that sort of miracle more than once seemed horribly naïve. Besides, her biggest fear now was giving the whole neighborhood food poisoning. They'd never be able to recover from a lawsuit.

She'd taken a gamble on the magically appearing pies and won, but that morning, they hadn't had anything else to lose. They were in a better position now, so was it worth the risk to tempt fate again?

That night, Frank slept like a baby, but she was nervous. Was it the beginnings of food poisoning in her grumbling stomach, or was it just that her stomach didn't remember what it felt like to be full? Maybe it was hunger. She regretted Frank giving away their last pie. Her mouth salivated at the thought of the delectable treat.

She became so obsessed with the scrumptious pastries. She could have sworn she smelled them again. Was she dreaming? No, she was quite awake. She sat up and realized she did, indeed, smell baking meat pies.

She dashed down the stairs to the shop, but when she burst through the back door, all she found were the pies and no evidence of who had made them.

Frank joined her about twenty minutes later, after she had eaten her fill of pies. His eyebrows rose in shock as he looked outside. The number of customers had doubled from the day before. Luckily, so had the number of pies.

They threw open their doors and let the tide in.

All day long, they heard nothing but compliments from all of the customers. Ones from the day before sang the praise of how delicious they had been, how they had dreamed of them all night long, and had then told their friends about them and brought them along. Jenna just smiled as they forked over their cash.

Near the end of the rush, she watched Frank out of the corner of her eye as he boxed up a whole baker's dozen worth pies. When the last customer rushed off, Frank gave her a nod.

"Gonna take these over to the local homeless shelter. I'm sure they could use a bite to eat."

Jenna sighed as he made his way out the door. The poor, simple, horribly misguided sap. She shrugged it off, though. They made enough to break even on all of their debts. One more day like this, and they might even make a profit.

That night she was uneasy again. Where, in this economy, was that quality of meat coming from? Who in their right minds would do work for the benefit of someone else with no recompense themselves? It just wasn't right. That night, after Frank had fallen asleep, she sneaked downstairs and hid so she could see the kitchen.

She had to stifle a scream when a line of little men, barely six inches tall, paraded across the kitchen counter with hunks of meat they tossed into the meat grinder.

Elves? She clamped her hands over her mouth to stifle a laugh or a scream. She wasn't sure which. Elves. Little helper elves.

God, they were hideous, though. Their bodies were twisted and misshapen. Their eyes glowed red, and their fangs were sharp and pointed. Demon elves, maybe. The worst part was they were completely naked. She watched in morbid fascination as they waved their tiny little elf-parts all over her kitchen. Surely that wasn't sanitary.

She clutched her knees to her chest, half-terrified and half-fascinated. She had to be dreaming. She'd wake up in the morning, and there would be a rational explanation.

If there was, she didn't find one. She woke up slouched against the wall, her whole body aching. The elves were gone, but the pies were made. Even more than the day before. Triple the amount of the first day. For some reason, though, she wasn't hungry for meat pies anymore, not after being exposed to the unsanitary practices of naked elves baking.

After the breakfast rush, she took the profits and went grocery shopping for lots of fruit and vegetables, but no meat.

As she made her way home, she found one of the Hoffman kids sobbing right outside the shop. Which one was it, Tommy or Timmy? Maybe the brat was hungry? She tried to channel Frank's inner Good Samaritan and invited him inside the shop for something to eat.

Tommy was his name, and he picked at his meat pie as he sniffled. Apparently the day before, the twins' cat, Tails, had gone missing, and when his brother Timmy had gone off after Tails, he'd disappeared as well.

Frank patted his shoulders comfortingly when Jenna expressed her concern.

"We'll definitely go to the police if he's gone for much longer. In the meantime, we'll keep an eye out for little Timmy and Tails, as well." Frank took another load of leftover pies to the soup kitchen across town. When he got home, Jenna hugged him tightly.

"Frank, will you stay up with me tonight? So we can see who is doing this for us?"

"Isn't that kind of like spying on Santa Claus?" he chided.

She suppressed a shudder. Decidedly not. "Don't you want to know who to thank? Today is the first day we've made a profit in this business for two years." More than that, she wanted to make sure she wasn't losing her mind. Surely little demon elves weren't their actual benefactors.

Frank sighed and stuffed his fist into a yawn. "I'll try to stay up for a little bit."

Frank nodded off before anything happened, but it didn't take much longer. As little as the men were, and as much meat as they had for the pies, they got started early in the evening. She elbowed Frank in the ribs, and he jolted awake. She shushed him and pointed.

He sat there next to her, hidden behind a stack of boxes, and watched wide-eyed as the elves threw huge chunks of meat into the grinder and cooked it into pies.

"I'll be damned," he whispered as he watched the little creatures work.

"God, but they're ugly," Jenna whispered back.

"It's not what's on the outside that counts," he shot back. "Just look what they are doing for us."

She rolled her eyes. *Pathetic sap.*

By the time the shop opened, heaps of pies were ready for the howling masses waiting for breakfast.

After the rush, Jenna sat at the counter while Frank swept up. There was no sign of the homeless man, the twins, or their cat, Jenna realized. She pushed a little pile of crumbs around until Frank came through and swept them away.

"Frank, where do they come from? And where do they get the meat?"

Frank frowned. "It's no good to question miracles."

"Well, I am questioning them. Good God, Frank, what if these little monsters are killing our neighbors to feed the rest of us? Hacking up their body parts and putting them into pies?"

Frank laughed. "You are letting your imagination run away with you, Jenna dear."

She wasn't convinced, especially when a sobbing Mrs. Hoffman came by looking for her boys. Frank consoled her by giving her a meat pie.

Jenna grimaced as the woman bit into it. What if her very own son had been butchered to make that particular pie she was eating?

She ran into the bathroom and threw up.

That night, she hid in the kitchen, waiting with dread for the elves to show up. They did. They ground up meat and made pies until she felt like she was going to throw up again, even though there was nothing left in her stomach.

Who was left? The whole homeless shelter? Mrs. Hoffman? Her and Frank themselves? She'd never sleep again. Or eat. Not as long as these little beasts invaded her kitchen every night.

⤞⋗⤝

She tried to shoo them away a couple different nights. They just shook their little fists at her and scurried away. But still, the pies were always waiting in the morning.

"You should stop staying up all night watching them, Jenna dear. You're looking a little ragged around the edges," Frank said after about a week. "Eat something, too. You've lost weight."

She glared at him and chewed on a finger. Her finger, not one of the fingers ground into meat pies. Frank bit into a pie, and juice spilled down his chin. She shivered, tried to suppress the nausea, but failed. She dashed to the bathroom.

She noticed Frank didn't bring pies to the homeless shelter anymore. When she asked him about it, he shrugged.

"It's the darnedest thing. They just don't get homeless folks there anymore. I've tried the soup kitchen, but their numbers are declining, as well. I guess maybe the economy is turning around. Or maybe the elves are helping everyone out."

She went upstairs, curled into a little ball, and cried herself to sleep. When Frank came to bed, she woke and took up her post in the kitchen, watching the elves.

How much longer could she keep on like this? The goddamned things were taking over her life, eating her whole town. Soon there'd be nobody left. One night, she tried attacking them, but they were too quick. After that, she started leaving ground meat for them to use, but they always brought and used their own. She locked the doors, boarded them up at night, and they still got in, still made their pies, and got out somehow.

She couldn't stop watching them work. Her eyes tracked their movements at all times. Their little bodies made her sick, those little elf penises dangling as they worked. If only they'd wear clothes. Even lunch ladies had to wear hairnets, for crap's sake.

The next day she went to the store and bought some doll clothes. She set them out on the counter next to the beef she left for them to use. She wasn't hopeful, but maybe they'd do her one courtesy.

Strangely enough, that night, when they arrived, they stopped short at the clothes. They exchanged glances, then dropped their bundles, threw their hands in the air, and screamed. The little bastards urinated on the clothes, and then took off running.

She shook her head. What the hell? The little things weren't afraid of her, but they fled in the face of clothing?

She went to bed, but clutched her best butcher knife, just as she had taken to doing for weeks now. She was surprised to find Frank wasn't in bed. Had he heard the ruckus downstairs and gone to investigate? She shrugged and sunk into bed, knife to her chest. Eventually exhaustion won out, and she fell asleep.

When she woke up, it was quiet, and there was a stale smell in the air. No smell of baking pies. That was a relief. Too good to be true, even.

No Frank in bed next to her, either. Was he up already?

She cautiously made her way downstairs. When she pushed through into the store, there were no pies. No pies anywhere. She went into the kitchen, and there were the pee-stained clothes she had left for the elves.

Clothes. What story had she heard that brought up some vague sense of familiarity at that? She couldn't remember, so she pushed the thought aside. Along with the soiled clothing, she found the bundles they had dropped. The meat they were going to make pies out of.

Taking a closer look, she jerked backward.

She tried to scream and couldn't. She realized she was still holding the butcher knife and dropped it. When it clattered to the ground, the sound shattered the frozen moment, and she did scream then.

She screamed until the police came and arrested her for the murder of her husband, whose body parts littered the kitchen.

They managed to tack on the murder of several other victims, including the Hoffman twins and a number of homeless folks, but managed to keep the story of the meat pies out of the press.

"That's just sick, lady. Why would you do it?" the arresting officer asked as he shoved her into a police car.

She shook her head and choked on a hoarse sob. They'd never believe her. She didn't even believe herself.

"It was the elves."

# LAKE TIVEDEN
*by MD Maurice*

The willows lining the lake cast ink black, ominous shadows on its surface. Peter tried to ignore them, but the way their weeping bows stretched out across the water toward his ramshackle boat that morning made him feel anxious and fearful.

The fisherman bent down to check the tautness in one of his lines and felt the telltale tremble along the thread signaling something was on the hook. He worked quickly, keeping a steady rhythm as he pulled the line up slowly, wrapping the slack around the spool as he went. As the catch neared the surface, Peter's heart fell. The fish was too small, not a keeper. He released it and watched it take off into the depths, the gold scales briefly flashing in the gloom before it disappeared.

Peter had been fishing for five hours with only two keepers so far. Yesterday it had been only four in nine hours. The lake was just not providing as it had for his father and his grandfather. He looked across the lake to where his trailer sat perched on the slight rise above it. How long had he survived this way? The money he made from fish was barely enough to keep the roof over their heads, even with his part-time cannery job. Greta would be heading back to school in a few months, and she would need clothes and supplies. He had no idea how he would make ends meet if the lake continued to deny him.

Peter's family, along with hundreds of others, had fished the massive lake for decades. They had raised their families on its shores and made a decent living from the fish and fowl living there. By the time it was Peter's turn at the helm, however, the years of pollution and over-fishing had made the lifestyle nearly impossible. One by one the families of the small fishing community had abandoned the lake.

The tiny trailer he had once shared with his wife Becca was now falling down around his and Greta's heads. He had to do something, or they would not make it. As he often did in times when despair threatened to overcome him, he closed his eyes and thought of his late wife. Becca had soft brown eyes sparkling above a delicate mouth that twitched with mischief and laughter. She was unfailingly and eternally hopeful. Even when the cancer had worn her down to skin and bones, she still teased him into boyish laughter with her quick wit.

Peter shook himself loose of his thoughts and tested more of his lines. He settled down in the bow. He knew it was going to be a long day yet, and he was already so very tired. As he often did in the quiet hours, he thought of Greta. She had her mother's beautiful red hair and flawless ivory skin. It brought him peace to gaze upon her loveliness, but it was her fierce, loyal heart and unwavering faith that gave him comfort beyond measure.

The waves lapping against the boat woke Peter up before the drop in temperature did. The surface of the lake was suddenly broiling with white caps, and the air was shrieking madly. The tips of his ears burned with the cold, and his hands were like ice inside his leather gloves. The weather in the wet season was prone to disturbances, but such a rapid swing was rare. Peter pulled in all the lines, noting with dismay that every single one was empty. He started for shore where the trees bent and swayed in the violent wind.

A hundred yards out, something big hit the bottom of the boat, killing the motor and pitching Peter overboard. He came up sputtering and reached for the side of his boat to haul himself up and out. Suddenly the chop around him stilled, and the pressure in the air dropped enough to make his ears pop. He pulled himself up enough to look across the bow of the boat. There, almost twenty feet off his stern, was a massive white shape just visible beneath the green-gray water. Before he could move, the shape rose up and broke the surface. An enormous white horse, its neck and mane streaked with dark lake mud, its dark opal eyes wide with terror, struggled in the waves. After a few agonizing seconds, its legs seemed to find purchase, and it surged forward toward shore. When it reached the shallow shelf, it stopped, belly deep in the water. It turned to gaze back at Peter.

The fisherman managed to get back in the boat and started the engine. He made slowly for the animal who still had not broken eye contact with him. As he got closer, he could not make out any visible injuries. He stopped several feet away. The skin on its flanks shimmered, beautifully translucent in the low light. Its great white mane whipped about in the wind, transparent as fog.

"Hey, boy, it's all right now." Peter reached out his hand.

The words rattled in Peter's throat as a deep voice ricocheted around his head, a voice that both terrified and comforted him. The voice compelled him with ripe promises and commanded him with unyielding authority. His entire body felt hot, as if he burned up inside. The vision of the horse flickered then shook in front of his eyes like a mirage. Peter tasted blood. He had somehow bitten his tongue and could feel his cheeks were wet with tears. The awful voice pounded in his head straining his eardrums. *This is not a horse*…he had the chance to think before the world went dark.

❧❧

Greta rolled out pie crusts on the kitchen counter. She loved the new house. She had her own room, and the wood floors were cool under her bare feet. Her father was still at the farmers' market. He said he wanted to pick up some extra cash, but she knew he had sent her home early because he wanted to go shopping alone for her birthday. She was going to be eighteen the next day. She'd start a new job inland working for a large horticulture firm in the city in two weeks. It was an exciting time, but Greta still worried about leaving her father alone.

It had been almost two years since that strange day he had returned from fishing. He had been soaked through and for weeks after had been at turns both oddly paranoid and defiant. She had found him several times, stalking along the shore and mumbling incoherently at the water. His flesh had been feverish, his eyes wild. She had been frightened and could not reach him, locked as he was, in combat with some invisible foe.

It had been a difficult few years for them both after Mom had died. They had nearly lost everything until it seemed Dad's luck had turned around. The sturgeon yield had been so good on the lake that he'd been able to cut back on his hours at the cannery. His health had improved as his stress level decreased. They were not wealthy by any stretch, but they were comfortable. Dad had been able to upgrade them from the broken-down trailer to a nice, cozy modular home with new amenities and a lovely garden out back for Greta to grow beautiful produce in. Her heirloom tomatoes and sweet peas were a big hit in the local markets, and it had given her extra money for the first time in her life. They were blessed.

❧

Peter hurried back out to the car, the present for Greta tucked tightly under his arm. He had been feeling oddly anxious all day, and he was eager to get home to his daughter. He was excited to see her face when he placed the new digital camera into her hands. He had a big speech prepared about not wanting her to miss a thing in the big city. Peter even had plans to have Greta sign him up for one of those silly sharing sites so he could see the all the photos she uploaded. The thought of her leaving shot a bolt of white hot panic across his heart. Peter hated to see her leave, but he was so proud of Greta, and he knew it was the life he and his wife had wanted for her. He set the new Nikon on the passenger seat and headed for home.

Peter had just turned onto the winding road leading down to the lake when he felt a sharp, hot pain in his gut. He cried out, wondering briefly if he was going to be sick. The lake had just become visible, and the surface of the water looked like it was boiling. Peter strained to get a better look and noticed it wasn't waves or chop but hundreds...no, thousands of fish breaking the surface. He stared incredulous at the enormous school, transfixed. His eyes traveled across the surface of the lake, and for far as he could see fat fish backs rolled and thrashed in the water.

Peter's eyes fell on something else, something impossible. Peter sprang from the truck. His entire body went rigid with fear. He bent at the waist suddenly and vomited dark volumes of lake water onto the tops of his boots. In the very center of the lake stood a massive white horse. As soon as Peter discerned its shape, it changed into something else, something horrific. The word came deep from the recesses of his mind, from that place of childhood night terrors and screaming wakefulness. Just one word, Nokken, the boogie monster of his nightmares, the same creature of the old tales told by fisherman over pints in foul-smelling ale houses. The Nokken was a creature of tremendous power. It had the power to strike bargains and deliver on dreams, but it did so at a terrible price.

The Nokken rose up from the water, a jagged, vaguely humanoid shape against the black sky. Its yellow, luminous eyes locked on Peter's, and it moved with alarming speed until it was just twenty feet from where he had fallen to his knees in the sawgrass. The smell of decay wafted around him, choking him with its fetid stink and making his eyes tear.

The mouth opened, a dark and terrible maw that seemed to shriek, though the only sound Peter heard was the beating of his own heart. Then the Nokken raised one arm, a rotting, slime-covered limb, and pointed a gnarly black finger at Peter. All at once he heard the voice in his head again, as he had before, compelling him.

"Give her to me."

Peter's nose began to bleed from both nostrils, and he swiped at it absently, straining to understand the Nokken's demand.

The language was garbled, but slowly it began to make sense. When the full message dawned on him, Peter screamed and shook his head so violently the blood from his nose became a fine mist. The Nokken nodded. It would be obeyed. Then it showed Peter what would happened if it wasn't. Images ran through Peter's head like an old filmstrip, the violence and gore so clear and vivid there was no question it would come to pass. Peter saw Greta's torn and eviscerated body lying on the shore of the lake. Rose-colored water pooled around her ruined form, her dead eyes stared up at the gray sky. Greta, poor Greta. Peter sobbed and tore at his shirt and hair. Out in the lake the Nokken nodded again, a deliberate and awful action as final as death to Peter, and sank into the depths.

It took Peter a long time to recover. He did so with a new and terrible clarity, a horrible explanation for all the recent good fortune. The Nokken had gifted Peter the lake's blessings and all that had come with it. The Nokken had given freely and now it wanted payment. It wanted Greta.

Peter had unknowingly entered into a pact with a demon and had used his own daughter for currency. He had not remembered before, but now he understood everything. Greta was turning eighteen, and the Nokken had come back to claim his prize. If Peter refused, the demon had promised a brutal death for Greta. It had shown it to him, inside his mind, like a snuff film from the darkest depths of hell. Greta had to come to the Nokken and offer herself willingly, or the monster would take her by all the force and pain at its disposal.

ॐ๛

Greta sat stone still as her father told her about the Nokken. He wept anguished tears, clasping her hands in his, begging her to forgive him. He had not known the terrible price she would pay for their fortunes. It seemed too immense for him to bear. Greta did not understand. At first, she thought he had been drinking or was having a breakdown of some sort. His story sounded like dark fantasy to her.

The Nokken was a silly legend, a monster to keep children quiet and fearfully respectful of the water. Don't wander too deep or the Nokken will get you. Mythical creatures could not walk on land, claim, and kill. The more her father talked, the more she understood there could be no truth to his prediction. He had finally worn himself out with the telling, and she put him to bed after several hearty glasses of brandy.

Should she call the doctor? She decided in the morning she would ring Dr. Earl and tell him about her father's episode. She wondered with a stab of guilt if it could have been brought on by the stress of her leaving him.

Greta had fallen quickly to sleep, exhausted with worry for her father, but her eyes flew open in the dark. There was something in her room, something dark and fetid standing just out of her line of sight. She tried to sit up, but found her limbs pinned to her sides. Her chest hurt with the effort of breathing. Something slid slowly up her body, the pressure of it against her skin, wet and cold. It rose up her bare legs. Frigid talons inched up her thighs, under her nightgown, rising past her hips. She heard a rasping sound like labored breathing, as it paused just above her navel. Something sharp raked her belly. Teeth?

She cried out in revulsion and fear. Greta's eyes were wide, straining to see through the inky blackness all around her, seeking to give form to what was on top of her. The smell stronger, dank and rotten, filled her nostrils and made her gag. Icy cold tendrils snaked up her sides and over her naked breasts, squeezing and clawing the tender flesh before closing in on her neck. She was stricken with terror. She struggled to breathe. The air above her grew thick, like swirling clouds of black smoke. Something horrific leaned down, parting the inky black vapor with its awful mass. The Nokken's sickly yellow eyes flashed with menace. It opened its jaws, exposing rows of jagged, razor sharp teeth. Blackness rolled over her.

≈∞

Peter rushed through the house to Greta's room. The sound of her screams had woken him, and he'd raced to find her sitting on the edge of her bed shaking uncontrollably. Without a word, he drew her to him. Her body was cold and smelled rank, like the bottom of the lake-bed. His daughter looked up at him, and the terrible understanding in her eyes made every cell in his body ache with dread. The Nokken had issued its one warning. Tomorrow evening, she would have to go to it or suffer a fate worse than either of them could ever imagine.

Peter and Greta worked tirelessly, pouring through all the literature they could find on the creature. They read every first-hand account, every legend, and every children's story that alluded to the beast. After a long day, Peter's face was gray and his eyes red-rimmed from crying. Greta slowly took his face in her hands and kissed him. Resigned to her fate, she wanted only to spend what little time she had left with her father. She begged him to walk with her in her garden. She held his hand and leaned against him. Greta was calm, comforted by the lush green garden with its wonderful earthen smells. Her father was grief-stricken, but soon he would have peace. Greta knew something he did not.

She had found an old story, and she believed it gave her to key to destroy the Nokken. It would require her sacrifice, but it would free her and her father forever. Tonight, when the Nokken came to the water's edge to claim her, it would be in its true form. Greta understood it was most vulnerable then, and she had but a few moments to act and rid the lake of its evil.

Death was what the Nokken had promised her, but her death would be its destruction.

෧•෧

Greta led Peter to the edge of the lake. The moon was impossibly full and bright. He had never thought his daughter to be more beautiful than she looked wrapped in its luminous glow. Her long red hair was tied back, framing her heart-shaped face. He held her, unwilling to believe he was about to lose her forever. He prayed his plan would work, that the Nokken would agree to take him instead. He had the offerings with him, a vial of his blood and the best bottle of brandy his money could buy. He would only have a few moments to make his plea. He hoped it would be enough to save his daughter from her terrible fate.

In the center of the lake the white horse broke the surface and moved toward them. Peter clutched Greta tightly. As the Nokken drew closer, it shifted shape into its true form. Its body became more human-like. It had a broad male torso draped with lake grass and covered in mud and detritus. Its head was massive, hung with thick ropes of black hair. There were few features in the blackness of its face, save for its glowing yellow orbs and wretched mouth stretched wide and filled with teeth like rows of needles. It stopped a few yards off and raised its arms out to Greta. She stepped forward, and it keened and moaned, a sound that turned Peter's blood to ice. He rushed forward, proffering the bag of offerings, grabbing Greta's arm and pulling her back.

The Nokken hissed and tossed the sack aside. It rounded on Peter, closing one claw-like hand around his throat and lifting him off the ground.

"Let her go you rotten son of a bitch," Peter sobbed before the Nokken's fist squeezed his throat.

Greta screamed as her father's feet flailed and kicked high above her head. She beat her fists frantically against the Nokken's back, begging it to spare her father. In desperation, Greta tugged off her dress, and threw her nude body against the Nokken, pressing her young inviting flesh against its dankness. In its male form, the creature was consumed by lust. With relief Greta saw it drop Peter with a heavy splash into the shallows. Greta screamed as the demon pulled her to his bare chest and covered her mouth with its own.

❧

Greta, fighting for her father's life as much as her freedom, locked her open mouth with the demon's, even as she felt the vile creature going hard against her body. The demon's thick and diseased tongue slipped inside her, sucking at her soul. She knew it was time. She wrapped her arms and legs around the creature, using all her strength to keep their bodies connected, mouth to mouth, flesh to flesh. Greta plunged the sharp, eight-inch blade as deep into her own chest as she could. The Nokken struggled to free itself from the dying girl. As Greta's lifeblood turned the waves red around them, the demon howled and screamed into her throat. It stumbled back, sinking into the silt. Greta clung, her arms tightening around its neck, as it dragged her down into death.

❦

Peter came to just in time to see his daughter locked in an impossibly obscene embrace with the Nokken. He watched as both of their bodies twisted and faded into transparency before sinking below the surface soundlessly.

He screamed, "No Greta, no!" in a long, agonized wail of torment.

He thrashed into the lake, diving again and again, looking for his daughter in the darkness. He searched all night until at last his body gave out, and he pitched forward on the shore. Greta was gone. She had sacrificed herself to save him, knowing only death itself would destroy a Nokken forever.

The sun was warm and comforting on Peter's face. He opened his eyes and slowly, painfully rose to his knees on the sand. The morning was absolutely beautiful before him. Peter gazed at the lake in front of him in astonishment, choking back tears. The entire surface of the lake, as far as his eyes could see, was covered by a blanket of the most exquisite red water lilies he had ever laid eyes on. The sun spread its rays over the flowers, lighting them like flames as they gently bobbed on the swells. The lilies were a deep and glorious red, the same lovely shade as his daughter's hair.

# WAX SHADOW
*by Emerian Rich*

"If you're just joining us, we have on set, the star of the *Iron Fist Commander* series, the highest grossing movie franchise in the last ten years. He can currently be seen Friday nights, battling the baddies on *Judge and Jury*, Mr. Josh Anton!"

The crowd roared as Josh put down his mug of water and smiled at the host of *Up Late*, Larry Sheldon.

"So, Josh I hear you brought a clip of your newest flick, *Iron Fist Commander 4*?" Larry asked as he gave a toothy grin to the audience.

"Yeah, no need for a setup."

"None?"

"Nope. Just me being a badass." The audience laughed on cue, most of them of the female persuasion.

"Okay, Sam, you heard him. Let it roll."

A massive flat screen television situated between Larry and Josh rolled up and the screen flashed with brightly colored, moving words that stated, "Exclusive Clip."

Samantha Winters appeared on screen in a tight leather dress with thigh-hi black lace-up boots. The men in the crowd whistled and hooted. The shot widened to reveal Josh grabbing onto a rope dangling from a helicopter up above. His normally unruly auburn hair was hidden under The Commander's usual black skullcap. His brilliant blue eyes stared out at the audience, dazzling them into awe before he slipped on his signature black shades.

"What do you mean you aren't going to tell me?" Samantha asked, hand on hip, the other clutching an impressive-looking machine gun.

"Like I said," he yelled over the helicopter's roar. "It's on a need to know." Wrapping the helicopter cable around his arm a few times, Josh held on as the helicopter moved away, him dangling from the cable with one arm, a black shotgun in the other.

"And I don't need to know." Samantha shook her head, a knowing grin replacing her skeptical scowl. "I hope you know what you're doing, Commander." Behind her, men on the roof closed in. She mowed them down with a sweep of the machine gun.

The shot cut back to Josh, crashing through the glass window of a top floor in a massive high-rise. He landed on his feet with guns in both hands. A room full of Japanese businessmen reacted to his entrance as the man at the head of the table stood.

"Commander." The man sneered, motioning for his goons to attack.

"Miss me?" Josh, as The Commander said, and the clip cut off.

The crowd went wild as Larry yelled over them. "There you have, it folks, Josh Anton!"

Larry shook Josh's hand and leaned in as they went to commercial break. "Great to have you on."

The second they were off air, Josh met Alan, his PA, backstage. Alan handed him bottled water.

"Great show. You've got about an hour to kill before we leave for the flight back to L.A."

"It'll be nice to get home." Josh winked at a pretty redhead as he walked toward his private dressing room.

"I put your favorite hoagie in the dressing room, and one of the interns is getting you a protein shake. Oh, the people from Star Experience called again."

"Who?" Josh opened his dressing room and unbuttoned his dress shirt. He downed half the water before retrieving deodorant from his bag.

"Star Experience. The people who want to make a life-size model of you that tourists can take pictures with."

"Oh, yeah." Josh took off his shirt and ran a hand through his hair.

"What shall I tell them?"

Standing in front of the mirror and putting on his deodorant, Josh grinned at himself. Sure, why wouldn't anyone want a statue of his body? He'd worked hard to maintain zero body fat, pure muscle rippling from bicep to abs.

"Call Marty. Have him draw up the contract. Tell him I'll do it on two conditions. First I want the same money I got from Universal, and second, I want one."

"What a life size statue of yourself?" Alan scoffed.

"Yeah."

"Won't that be creepy?"

"Nah. I'll put it in my Malibu house. It'll be great." Heck, he could probably sell it on eBay for a couple mil if things got tough.

"Okay, anything else?"

"Yeah," Josh said. "Make sure the redhead brings me the shake and text me when the car is here."

"Will do, boss," Alan said before leaving him alone in the dressing room.

❧

The human-sized box arrived about a month after Josh had gone in for measurements. Alan had it unpacked and waiting to greet him when he came home to his Malibu beach house from his studio shoot.

Josh dropped his bag in the pristinely white foyer and removed his sunglasses, staring into his twin's eyes. The resemblance was uncanny. The sculptors had recreated him flawlessly.

"He came naked. I hope you don't mind I dressed him in one of your T-shirts and jeans."

Josh lifted his double's black T-shirt and admired the abs. He lifted his own T-shirt and smiled. Up higher, on the statue's left pec an imprint of the familiar Star Experience logo was branded into his flawless skin. Josh admired his forearms and lower. A thought struck him as he looked to his double's filled out jeans. Did they equip him with everything? He looked at Alan, a brow raised.

"Oh, he's not anatomically correct. They molded the black boxers attached."

Josh grinned sheepishly. "I wondered why they measured my inseam in my boxers."

Josh's girlfriend, Jill, walked into the house. "Oh, Lord, as if you weren't in love with yourself enough already." Her long, tan legs caught his eye as they led his gaze to her short skirt covering a perfect ass he ached to touch. "Now you have a life size doll to play with. If they gave him female parts you wouldn't even need me."

"I'd rather touch your female parts." Josh grabbed her ass and pulled her into him, a deep kiss earning him her enthusiastic participation. Alan made himself scarce as Josh pushed Jill into the wall separating the foyer from the rest of the house. She moaned as he ran his hand over her breast, and she wrapped her legs around him.

"Missed you," she gasped as he finally let her go.

"Let's catch up." He threw her over his shoulder and headed for the bedroom as she squealed in mock distress.

❦

Josh woke to a noise somewhere outside. Leaving Jill to sleep, he got up and grabbed a police baton he'd taken from one of his movie sets. The house was dark, and he journeyed down the hall to make sure Alan had set the alarm before he left. Through the front windows, he admired the view. Small waves rolled in, a line of glittering moonlight leading the way to the deserted sand. He stepped over to the foyer and flinched, before he remembered the dark looming figure of a man was his double. A nervous laugh eased the beating of his heart, and he inspected the alarm panel, where a green light blinked happily, denoting that all was well.

The dim light coming in through the window beside the door, glinted in his double's eye. He flicked on the entry-way light, thinking he'd leave it on for the rest of the night. Looking over Josh2 the resemblance really was uncanny. From the slight wrinkle near his eyes when he smiled, to the scar on his chin he'd received while filming the first Commander movie.

Retrieving a glass of milk from the fridge, Josh headed back to the bedroom, nodding at his body double as he passed the foyer.

"Keep an eye out for me, will ya, buddy?"

&#8734;&#8734;

The *Iron Fist Commander 4* premiere left Josh with an uneasy feeling. Sure, the movie was well received, and he killed on the red carpet, but as he watched, he wondered if he'd be doing Commander movies for the rest of his life. How could he keep going at such a pace with his TV series, the movies filming every summer, and public appearances? It wasn't just what people saw on TV, but also the six days in the gym every day and training in martial arts on top of that. After going over his calendar with Alan that morning, he felt overwhelmed. No one could keep up the pace and survive. He needed a vacation bad. He was tired. He'd been tired for weeks, and that didn't normally happen to him. He'd had an insatiable thirst for high octane sports and activity his whole life. Maybe he was coming down with something.

"Where to next?" Jill asked, pumped from the after party and ready to make their usual rounds at the VIP sections of their favorite clubs.

"Home."

"Ohh…" She slung her leg over his lap and ran her hand over his chest. "Is the Commander in need of a massage?"

"No." He swiped her hands down, onto her own lap. "I need some sleep. I'm exhausted."

"Oh." Jill pulled back, sitting next to him with a concerned frown crossing her perfect face. "Are you okay?"

"Yeah. I'm just…I might be coming down with something."

"Poor, baby. Okay, I'll come tuck you in. Make you some soup."

"No." He leaned back, resting his head as he closed his eyes. A headache was coming on. "I just need silence and my bed."

"Um, okay." She acted like a hurt puppy, but he had no energy to console her.

"You go. Take the car. Pick up Becky. Use my VIP pass." He fished the black metallic card out of his wallet and put it in her hand.

"If you're sure." She held in her excitement, but he knew she would forget about him the moment he got out.

"I am. I just need some downtime." He kissed her on the forehead as the car pulled up to his house.

Josh waved as Jill left to party with her best friend. Entering his beach house, Josh sighed. His twin's bright smile met him as he passed Josh2 in the foyer. He took off his jacket and hung it over the figure's shoulders.

"Hold on to that for me, will ya?"

He envied the guy. Always in pristine shape, without the hours at the gym. Happy, never exhausted or upset, smile frozen in place, eyes always twinkling.

It exhausted Josh to look at him. Before falling asleep that night, he thought how nice it would be to stay at home for a few days. If only someone could take his place for a week, like that *Multiplicity* movie.

The next morning, and into the next week, Josh woke unsatisfied and without energy. He pushed through filming as it was the last week before a short hiatus on his TV show. On Friday morning, he sat in his trailer, dreading the fight scene to come. He'd just have to make it through. Gobbling an energy bar and protein shake, he scrolled through his phone.

Jill had been calling and texting to meet up, but he just didn't have the energy. Josh dialed his older brother instead. David was a doctor in Calabasas. Maybe he'd know what was going on.

"Well, if it isn't my big-shot movie star brother."

"Hi, Dave."

"Aren't you hanging off a cliff somewhere?"

"No." Josh smiled despite himself. They didn't talk much anymore, but he still loved his brother's sense of humor. "I'm in L.A."

"To what do I owe this pleasure?"

"I was wondering if you'd mind coming out to the beach house this weekend?"

"Having a big party? I know, you need waiters, right?"

Josh laughed. "No, I'm just…I'm not feeling well."

"What's wrong?" For the first time, David's voice took on a serious tone.

"I have no energy."

"How long?"

"A couple weeks."

"All right. I'll be down this afternoon after the traffic calms. It'll be good to see my baby brother again."

As Josh hung up, Alan popped his head in. "Ready for makeup?"

"Yeah, send her in."

"There's a sub. Samantha had a family emergency." Alan entered the trailer with a tall spindly guy behind him. He was pale, with ebony-lined eyes, making him appear like the live-action version of Jack Skellington. Just what he needed, a goth makeup artist.

"Don't make me too pale. Alan, show him the still."

Alan and Skellington looked at the shot from a few days before on Alan's phone.

"Geez, Josh…you might want to tan a few times on vacay." Alan bit his lip as he compared Josh with the photo. "Are you feeling all right?"

"I'm fine." Josh shoved the phone out of his face.

"Well, you'll have two weeks to rest up before shooting." Alan turned to Skellington. "Mr. Workaholic is finally getting some R and R, which means I get some, too."

"Listen, I need quiet," Josh said.

"Sure." Alan motioned to Skellington, and he put in his earbuds and opened his makeup kit.

Alan left, and Josh closed his eyes, running through the coming fight scene in his head as Skellington worked on his makeup.

&❧&

David showed up just after seven, doctor bag in hand. The brothers embraced.

"Geez!" David patted Josh on the back briskly. "I've seen the muscles on screen, but look at you!"

Josh laughed, a blush creeping up his cheeks. He never got nervous, but somehow hearing his older brother compliment him caused the little brother in him to blush. The pride of David was something he'd always craved since he was a child.

"Come in. Want a beer?"

"Sure, I'm off duty, and what Helen doesn't know…" David's wife Helen came with labels, conservationist, humanitarian, vegan, gluten-free, and non-alcoholic. It was pretty bad when his straight-laced brother was the rebel in his family.

"What is that?" David jumped, staring at Josh2 in disbelief.

"A wax figure made by Star Experience. I'm in thirty-two cities across the globe now."

"Really? The kids love that place." David edged closer, closing one eye and inspecting the dummy. "They even got the scar I gave you from pushing your bike too hard."

"Yeah." Josh laughed, subconsciously touching his right eyebrow where the scar cut it in half. He went into the kitchen, and David followed.

"Wild. I don't think I could handle looking at myself every day. It takes a particular sort of man to face that."

Josh popped the top of two beers, and they took seats at the breakfast bar stools.

David set his med bag on the table.

"Well, let's get the business out of the way." He pulled a stethoscope out of his bag and put it on. "How do you feel now?"

"The same. Tired. Even with a full night's sleep, I've got no energy."

"Um-huh." David listened to his heart and then took his blood pressure. "Heart is strong. No diet changes? New medications or vitamins? Supplements?" he asked suspiciously.

"No."

"Damn, I was sure those guns were due to steroids. I think you got the good genes."

Josh chuckled. "No, just a lotta hours at the gym."

"You've exercised as normal? No more, no less?" David ran his hands behind Josh's ears, and his thumbs pushed on either sides of his throat.

"Sure. It's been tough, feeling this way, but I've been pushing through."

"Any other symptoms?"

"No."

"Open up." David shone a light into Josh's mouth and held a tongue depressor in his other hand. "You know the rule. Put down your tongue, and I won't use the stick."

"Yes, Dad." Josh did as told, sitting still while David looked into his mouth and ears. In a lot of ways, David was like their doctor father. Dad had died years ago, but Josh still remembered trips to his practice and the smell of disinfectant and Band-Aids.

"Hmmm…" David took off his stethoscope and put his tools in his bag. "I'll need to see your blood tests before I know for sure, but I don't see anything apparently wrong with you." David checked his watch. "We've got just about thirty minutes till the lab closes, let's get the blood drawn now. You might just need some vacation. How long has it been?"

Josh sighed. "Years."

"When is your next break?"

"I've got two weeks before filming."

"Then I prescribe a steak dinner out with your brother and back early for a good night's sleep. You should also relax tomorrow. Sleep in. Heck, sleep for days if you need to. You've earned it."

By the time they got back to the beach house, Josh felt a little better, no doubt due to the family time.

"I'm gonna crash in your guest room and leave in the morning," David said. "I won't wake you. I'll call you when the test results come in."

"Thanks, Dave." Josh gave his brother a loose hug and then went to his own room to sleep. David was probably right, he just needed a break.

❧❦

Hearing the front door shut the next morning, Josh rolled over, moaning as he felt his throat sore. Oh man, it was official. He was getting a cold. *Damn it.*

He got up and went to the kitchen for a drink. Before he got there, he found Josh2 in the hallway, blocking his way to the kitchen.

"Funny, Dave." Josh rolled his eyes and moved the statue back by the door. After a drink, Josh went back to bed. For once, he was going to take David's advice to heart. No matter how luxurious it felt, he needed rest. He'd try not to think of the catch-up workout sessions he'd have to squeeze in before shooting.

❧

For the next few days, Josh was rarely lucid. He slept, he ate, and he had fever dreams, but didn't fight it. The cold would pass in a few days, and if not, he'd call David again.

Monday, his cell rang and he rolled over. *Jill.* He'd been avoiding her for long enough. He'd need to answer or she'd be calling the cops.

"Jill?" he croaked out.

"Poor, baby. So you really got sick, huh?"

"Yeah."

"I'll bring you soup."

"No. Stay away. I don't want you to get it." He didn't feel like having company at the time.

"Don't be silly. I'll wear a mask…a nurse outfit, it will be great."

"No, I…"

"Be right over."

"Jill? Jill?" Josh tossed his phone in the general direction of the nightstand. *Damn it.* He didn't want company. He didn't want anything but to be left alone.

Sometime later, his phone rang again. *David.* Josh's voice barely roughed out a syllable before a coughing fit overtook him.

"Ah, the pleasant sounds of sickness," David quipped.

"Yeah."

"I won't keep you. Your test results all came back normal. You probably know you have a cold by now. Get some rest. Call me when you recover. I'd love to see my brother regularly."

"Thanks, Dave. I will."

"Okay, go back to sleep. Doctor's orders."

❧

Must have been mid-week when Jill called again. Josh's voice was better, but he still didn't have energy to entertain her, even if she did all the work. His libido just wasn't awake yet, and that was strange. He'd been a sexual animal since about thirteen.

"Hey, how's my little patient doing?" Jill was on speaker phone, driving with the top down it sounded like.

"Exhausted."

"That was quite a burst of energy you had, considering."

"Huh?"

"All I'm saying is I need to wear that outfit more often."

"Whatever… I'm tired, Jill… just don't call me for a while, okay?"

"I don't understand. Didn't you have a good time?"

He had no energy to answer.

"Josh? Baby?"

He hung up. Next week. He could make it up to her next week.

෧෨

Hearing something in the kitchen, Josh tried to open his eyes. They didn't want to crack, but concentrating, he finally got them open to slits. The room was dim. It appeared to be late afternoon, or…dawn? He couldn't tell. Taking a deep breath, he realized his bladder was full to bursting. He got up, muscles aching as he slowly made it to the bathroom. God, he felt like an old man and looked like one, from the reflection in the bathroom mirror. He'd have to go tanning before the shoot.

Taking a shower, he loved the feeling of the warm water running over his sore muscles. He felt as if he'd run a marathon, but in reality, he'd not moved in days. *Atrophy*. The word swirled around in his head. Yes, he'd heard of that. Non-use of his muscles could cause them to become stiff and immovable.

Drying off, he decided he'd have a run after eating. Enough laying around. Some exercise would do him good. Checking the expiration on the milk, he downed half the bottle. He grabbed a banana, admiring its crispness as he bit in. He hated

143

the browning ones. Putting the milk back, he saw new veggies and meat in the fridge. Jill must have replenished or the maid. The place did look surprisingly clean for him being sick all week.

Josh went out the back of the house, admiring his infinity pool as he walked down the steps and out the gate to the beach. He ran near the water where the packed sand made it easier. Dangerous waves crashed against the shore in the setting sun. Not one surfer braved the deadly breakers. Side-stepping a bird that fought to dislodge a hermit crab from its shell, Josh felt a pop at the back of his left leg. Pain shot into his foot and up through his knee as his left leg buckled underneath him.

"Shit!" Crouching in the wet sand, Josh tried to massage his calf muscle without causing more pain. It was his own fault. He'd been so out of sorts. He forgot to stretch. He hobbled a few feet to a small rock formation where waves crashed on one side.

Staring down the beach, he wondered how he'd make it back to his house. Giving himself a pep talk, he scowled as he tried to stand.

"Damn it!"

"You all right there?" An older man in a baseball cap and sweats approached. Josh recognized him immediately. *George Sullivan*, the Josh Anton of thirty years prior. He'd been the star of an action series that topped even *Iron Fist Commander*'s popularity. Josh had been a fan since practically birth and knew he lived near him, but had never been lucky enough to meet him before.

"Wow, George Sullivan. I'm a big fan."

"Nice to meet you."

George held out his hand for a shake. Josh took it and shook, feeling the bigness of the moment as his heart raced. Although Josh was quite a fit guy who could beat most mortal men to a pulp, George's hand dwarfed his.

"Josh, right?"

Josh grinned. "Yes." Pain shot up his leg as he adjusted on the rock.

"Looks like you need some help, huh?"

"Unfortunately, I think I pulled my calf muscle."

George inspected his calf and nodded. "You'll probably be down for a while. Here, let me help you." George offered an arm and helped Josh up.

"Thank you."

"Which way is your place?"

"Down there, the gray fence." Josh pointed to his home which seemed like a few miles away to his aching leg.

"All right, you ready?" George placed his arm around Josh's back and braced against him. "Just try to walk as best you can. No rush."

Every concept of pain Josh thought he knew was tossed into the waves as he half-hobbled, and half-dragged himself home with the help of his childhood idol. When they got to the stairs, Josh eyed them with trepidation. How could he? Not wanting to show weakness, he took one step at a time, but on the third one, his leg seized up, and he fell back into George's grasp. George seamlessly picked him up and carried him to the door. The few minutes it took for the blinding pain to cease weren't long enough to hide Josh's embarrassment at being carried into the house by the bigger man. He'd never been so ashamed in his life. George set him on the couch and then wandered deeper into the house, coming back with ice packs.

Red-faced Josh didn't look up at his idol, he just muttered, "Thank you."

George ignored his embarrassment as he helped Josh prop up his leg on the sofa. Once Josh was settled, had a bottle of water and his cell phone next to him, George sat opposite him and took off his baseball cap, smoothing his graying hair back.

"Um, thank you again," Josh said, still running through the embarrassing scene in his head.

"Sure. What are neighbors for? I live three houses to the left. Blue awning. Come on over if you ever run by and see me at home."

Josh couldn't respond. Was George Sullivan actually inviting him over to his house? The ego in him kicked in before he said something stupid. *Of course he is. You're the top dog now.*

"After you've healed, of course."

Josh let out a nervous laugh. "Ha. Right."

"As long as you're set—you have someone to call to help, right?" George stood, edging toward the door.

"Yeah."

"All right then." George looked up, past Josh, to the foyer. He froze.

Josh looked to where he stared and realized it was Josh2 he was staring at. Oh God, he realized for the first time how tacky it was to have a statue of himself in his own house.

"Star Experience," Josh said, trying to play it off casually. "They sent me one." Now he was lying to his idol.

George's focus snapped back to Josh. "Yeah, I used to have one years ago."

"You did?" Interesting...his idol had been young and cocky once too? "What happened to him?"

"Um, you know, I'm not sure." George's awkward expression was replaced by a smile Josh knew he put on for the press. "Nice to meet you, kid. Take care."

Josh watched him go out the back door and disappear onto the beach. Wow. George Sullivan. Who would have thought he'd meet him like that? Josh looked back at Josh2. Yes, he should get rid of him, if only because he creeped everyone out who visited. Maybe at least move him into the game room downstairs.

As the house lay in quiet stillness, Josh's exhaustion attacked him, and he couldn't help but sleep.

❧☙

The sound of his doorbell woke him early the next morning. Josh moaned, rolling over and instantly regretted it as pain shot up his leg. The doorbell rang again, and a third time before he heard the door open. Oh good, it must be Jill, and she used her key, just when he needed her.

"Hello," a familiar voice said.

"Package for Josh Anton."

Josh sat up, twisting so he could see the doorway. There were two men. One in a brown delivery uniform and one—in his clothes?

"What the hell?" Josh said.

The delivery man looked past the man, at Josh's exclamation.

"Thank you," the man said, handing the delivery guy back his pad and stylus. He shut the door and turned to Josh. "Hello, Josh, how are you feeling?"

"Wha-what…" Josh stared into his own eyes. Josh2 had somehow come alive.

"I figured I'd answer because you can't walk. How did that happen? You hurt yourself on set?"

"No, I pulled my calf muscle running—wait. How are you talking? Am I dreaming?" He pinched himself, but realized, no, if he were dreaming, his leg wouldn't hurt so badly.

"I don't know, actually. I just woke up when you were sick. I don't have control over when I speak, which is why I didn't introduce myself before. Josh Anton, nice to meet you." He held out his hand to Josh and blinked innocently.

"You aren't Josh Anton! I am!"

"Right. So am I."

"No, no…you are a…a…dummy. A statue. Statues don't come alive."

"Hmm… I did." Josh2 shrugged. "Want some breakfast? I feel like a Denver omelet. You?"

Josh stared after him as he helped himself to Josh's kitchen and began to cook. He tried to wrap his head around it. How had Josh2 come alive? Was there some kind of magic in the wax? Was this an elaborate hoax by his brother?

"Who are you really?"

"Josh, come on, you're being an idiot. I'm you. From Star Experience, remember?"

Josh stared. How could a dummy come to life? Josh2 rolled his eyes and then took off his T-shirt. He came over to Josh and flexed his pectoral muscle.

"See?" Displayed prominently on Josh2's chest was the flesh colored, raised indent of the Star Experience branding. Josh reached for the mark, running his hand over the skin that felt like scar tissue.

"Hey! Hands off." Josh2 backed up, grabbing his T-shirt and putting it back on. "I'm not in for any self-love if you know what I mean. I don't think I was brought to life for that purpose."

Revulsion rose in Josh's gut. "I wasn't coming on to you, dumbass."

"Wouldn't blame you." Josh2 flexed his bicep and grinned. When he saw Josh wasn't impressed, he shrugged and continued to prepare breakfast.

Was he seriously that annoying? If he could rise, he'd deck him.

"I don't know why you're so worried about this. You need a break. I'm here to give you one. Just chill. What happened to the easy-going Josh Anton we all know and love?" Josh2 smirked.

Josh took a deep breath and ran his hands over his face. It was true, he'd never been so uptight in his life.

"Eat your breakfast." Josh2 handed him a plate Josh could've prepared himself. It was his famous Denver omelet. He took the plate, inspecting Josh2. He knew everything Josh knew. He was an exact replica in form, so why not just relax and let him pick up the slack for a while? At least until his leg healed and he got over whatever flu he was recovering from.

༺✦༻

For the rest of his vacation, Josh nursed his leg. It seemed to be getting better, and he appreciated Josh2's help. He cooked and cleaned, and it felt nice having a friend. It had been a long time since he had someone who shared his interests around him, someone he wasn't worried about being his friend only because of the money.

First day of shooting dawned, and Josh was able to rise and get ready without much pain. He still felt a lingering tiredness from his cold, but that would fade as he got back into his normal routine.

"What are you doing up?" Josh2 asked as Josh came into the kitchen with a slight limp.

"It's the first day of filming."

"I thought you were still in pain."

"Nothing a few pills won't fix." He downed a couple ibuprofen as Josh2 studied him.

"If you're sure, but, Josh, have you looked in the mirror recently? You aren't looking your best. I mean, you're a tan or two from being seen in public."

"I'm fine. Maybe a little pale, but it will be fine." Josh downed a glass of milk and ate a banana as Josh2 rinsed his breakfast plate.

Josh pulled on his jacket and slipped his keys and wallet into the pockets.

"What are you going to tell them about your leg?"

"I'll tell them I pulled it running, which I did. Now, out of my way."

"I'm not sure that's the best course of action, Josh." Josh2 held his hand out, blocking Josh's path.

"Look, I've appreciated your help and everything, but I have to start living my life again. Now, let me by."

The men stared, identical eyes searching each for weakness. Josh2 glanced away first. "Let me get the door for you." Josh2 went ahead and opened the door for him. He held his right hand outside, the sun shining on it as he smiled. "Nice weather. You won't need that jacket."

Josh pulled off one arm and then the other. His right hand felt numb. The jacket fell from his grip, but Josh2 grabbed it before it hit the floor.

"Whoa…you okay buddy?"

Dizziness came over him as he tried to move his hand. A searing pain gripped his chest. Hell, was he having a heart attack? He gripped the burning in his chest and fought of a wave of nausea.

"I really think it's best that I go in your place today." Josh2 took a step back, slipping on his jacket. "You know, until you feel better."

"But I…" The pain scorched, and Josh lifted his shirt to see molded skin, like he'd been burnt, or was it a mark of some kind? "What the hell?"

"Don't worry. I'll take care of it for you. Rest."

"Josh2, damn it, get back here!" Josh hobbled to the door, his leg stiffening as he walked. He grabbed hold of Josh2's jacket—*his* jacket.

Josh2 stuck his right foot out the door, and Josh tried to go after him, but his right leg stiffened as if it were cemented to the foyer floor.

"Get back here!" Josh yelled. As his hand numbed, the jacket's cloth pulled from it because he had no way to grab harder.

"Sorry, buddy, it's my turn." Josh2 stood outside the door and looked back in at him.

Josh tried to run after him, to move, to scream, to even blink, but he was frozen in the foyer, in the same stance as Josh2 had been.

# WITHOUT FAMILY TIES
*by Chantal Boudreau*

*I'm too old for this,* Jojo thought as he labored away in the candlelight, his dark eyes tired.

He had been the eldest of three siblings. Now he was the last of them. His life had already been one plagued by loneliness, but now he was truly alone. His younger brother, a construction worker living half a nation away, had fallen victim to a workplace accident. The middle-aged man and his wife had been childless at the time disaster had struck.

Jojo's sister had died from cancer before that, without ever marrying or having children out of wedlock. He believed that wouldn't have happened had she trusted in his magic, but she had chosen to separate herself from such things at an early age, embracing the culture of their new home country entirely. He could have evoked a *nkondi* to cure her sickness, but she had no interest in his type of healing. When she finally admitted her modern medical doctors had failed her, there had been no time to rescue her from death.

Jojo, on the other hand, had never turned away from the old ways, perhaps because he was the eldest. His sister would have told him to leave old world business to those who still lived there and better understood it, but he could not forget where he had come from. He had learned what he knew of *banganga* magic before emigrating, and even though he had not completed his teachings, it was not a calling easily abandoned. He had too much connection to the *bakisi* to walk away from the spirits and the power they could lend him. He also was too dedicated to his family line to ignore them now.

Interfere he would. This was why Jojo toiled late into the night. He used the candle he had lit for more than just mood and illumination. He also needed fire to invoke the *nkisi* he was creating, a substitute for family. Unfortunately, his wife had died in childbirth along with their first baby, another incident he blamed on modern medical doctors, and Jojo had chosen to refocus his life on being a *banganga* rather than remarrying.

That didn't prevent him from feeling loss every day of his sad life. In fact, it had become an obsession.

"I can't find another wife now," he muttered as he applied red ochre and charcoal to the construct fabricated from wood, clay, and fabric scraps. He paused to touch his silvering black hair and wrinkled brown skin.

*No young woman would have me, and a woman my age would be past the point of childbearing. Besides, I would make a terrible husband, set in my ways as I am. But I need a child—blood of my blood. Without offspring, there will be no future for my family. I can't let our bloodlines end with me even if it means turning to darker magic. I must work with the* bakisi *to find another way.*

Jojo propped up the wooden boy before him in order to add the final elements of his ritual. First was the *ovana*. His mother had passed the quartz stones down to her daughter, but Jojo's sister had stopped wearing them under her tongue when she had turned away from the old ways. Perhaps that was why all of the siblings had been left childless, their family's future still trapped within the stones. Jojo chose to nestle the *ovana*, the stones that represented his family's life essence and fertility, inside the mouth he had hollowed out for the doll, sealing them in with a leather tongue.

Last came his own contribution in an attempt to finalize his creation, a part of him sacrificed to make the doll truly a representation of his own offspring. He pierced the dark flesh of his hand with a ritual blade and watched the blood flow. He painted the doll liberally with it, the crimson liquid seeping into the wood as he did so.

"Blood of my blood." The invocation was spoken.

Wrapping his wounded hand when done, he eyed the doll thoughtfully. His son would need a name. Jojo smiled. He suddenly had the perfect one in mind.

"I will call you Berko. First child." A suitable name for Jojo's ultimate aspiration.

❧◈❦

"Got your own personal Pinocchio, I see," Stan said with a mocking laugh. The man who owned the tobacco product store that neighbored Jojo's own business—one offering African art and ritual items—would sometimes drop in to make crude or racist remarks. Jojo knew the man meant to be friendly, but instead was both offensive and annoying.

"I am no Geppetto," Jojo replied without looking at his neighbor. Stan's puppet reference had not been lost on him. "And this is no toy. It is a *nkisi*. It serves a higher purpose."

The fact Jojo kept Berko close to him as he rearranged some of the merchandise on his shelves was no doubt what had prompted Stan's remark, this and the fact most people couldn't tell the difference between *minkisi* and simple dolls. The intrusive neighbor wouldn't be able to differentiate a ritual mask from a decorative one, either.

The annoying man shrugged. "Looks like a wooden boy to me."

Jojo watched Stan leave, grateful for his departure. He placed Berko gently onto a countertop.

"I *know* you are more than that. You are my family's last remaining hope. You just need to build on the power I've given you to manifest yourself into living form."

*I* will *be a real boy someday, but I lack sufficient* mpungo. *That will be rectified in time.*

Jojo was startled at first by the voice in his head, but realized it made sense that Berko would communicate with his creator using such magical means until he had a proper voice of his own. The *nkisi* was, after all, infused with his blood.

"The *mpungo* I lent you is not enough?" Jojo asked.

He thought Berko would eventually manifest based on the magic of his spirit alone. That was how the spell was supposed to work if he had gotten it right.

*You are old, and I need to be young. Much of your magic is spent, Father, but don't fret. I'll find a way to make it happen. The power is out there to be reaped. I just need the proper source and the proper tools.*

Jojo found the idea disturbing, his blood running cold at the thought. He wasn't sure what Berko had in mind, but he doubted it was anything good.

"That's not necessary, Berko. If you need more power, I will find a way to source more for you. I want you to promise me you will not leave this shop of your own accord. I demand it."

Jojo knew that *nkisi* had to obey their *banganga* maker. Berko would oblige him.

*"I promise, Father."*

Something about the widening of Berko's ochre smile accompanying his words unnerved Jojo. So much so that rather than taking the *nkisi* with him, the *banganga* decided to leave the store that evening without the ritual doll. Jojo had research to do, and since Berko had agreed to not leave the shop without him, keeping him there would be best. Jojo wouldn't have to worry what might happen while he was otherwise occupied if he left the *nkisi* there. Berko would be safe while locked away in the store, as would everyone else.

❧❧

Berko sat silently in the dark after Jojo had gone, serenaded only by the crickets the old man kept in a jar to be used as ritual components. A real boy would have been frightened by the eerie shadows and lilting cricket cadence, but not Berko. *Nkisi* knew no fear.

This also meant that Berko did not start or panic when intruders broke their way into the store. The street thugs were not mere vandals but proper thieves hoping to find cash, jewelry, or other readily liquidated merchandise.

Disappointed to find all the money had been safely stowed away in a safe, the two young men, one bearing a tattoo of a wolf and the other of a tiger, grabbed anything which looked easily portable and somewhat appealing. Perhaps they could pawn the things for a meager reward.

Berko was one of those things.

Despite their rough handling, the *nkisi* was grateful to find himself stuffed into their bag. Because the intruders were choosing to steal him, this meant that Berko was able to leave the store without doing so of his own accord and therefore had not disobeyed his maker. He had not asked to be taken, even though he had been liberated in the process. As a result, Berko was free to go wherever he pleased. He would be able to fulfill his intended purpose.

When the street thugs arrived at their lair, they emptied out their bags to assess their ill-gotten goods. Berko tumbled out amongst the other masks, statuettes, and dolls the thieves had selected from the store's available merchandise. Tiger-tattoo picked up the *nkisi* and made a face.

"Why did you take this one? This is the ugliest doll I've ever seen! We'll get shit from the pawn shop for this."

Wolf-tattoo shrugged. "I took a likin' to the little fellow. I figured if we couldn't pawn him, I could keep him."

"I thought we agreed no souvenirs. Too risky. We don't want to keep anything that can link us to the crime. Besides, that thing's beyond ugly. If you keep it, it'll give me nightmares. Shove it back in the bag with the others. Maybe we can get some spare change for him."

When Wolf-tattoo did not act, Tiger-tattoo made a grab for Berko. The *nkisi* scrambled back, avoiding the young man's lunge, his first and only movement that expended some of his precious *mpungo*.

The thief gaped at him. Tiger-tattoo back-pedaled. "Did you see that? It moved."

"No way, you missed it and knocked it over with your clumsy paw."

Wolf-tattoo scooped Berko up and with a laugh wiggled the *nkisi* at his cohort in a mocking way, speaking for the ritual doll in a high pitched voice.

"What - you don't like me? You think I'm ugly? Well, I'll show you. You're just a big scaredy-cat. You should be afraid of lil' ole' me, you big pussy, 'cuz I'm going get you!" Wolf-tattoo then jabbed at his companion with the *nkisi*, uttering, "Nyah!" with each gesture and making Tiger-tattoo jump.

With the third, "Nyah!" and jab, Berko sourced some of Jojo's *mpungo* to will his nose to grow into a sharp, solid point - one that extended far enough to pierce Tiger-tattoo's breast and his heart. The *nkisi* quickly drank in the young man's *mpungo*, fresh blood coating wood, fabric, and clay along with what Jojo had already put there.

Once Wolf-tattoo realized what had just happened, he yelped and tossed Berko to the floor with a panicked, "What the fuck?"

Berko had already willed his nose back to its original form. While the magic flowed strong in him, he still did not have enough *mpungo* to manifest as a real boy. He needed more.

The *nkisi* lay still on the floor, blood-spattered and smiling his silent mirth with ochre ornament. Wolf-tattoo stared at his fatally-wounded friend, wringing his hands and running them through his hair as he paced his helplessness. The only sound accompanying his panic was a quiet, "Shit, shit, shit, shit, shit," eventually ending with a pleading, "I didn't mean to do that man. You got to believe me."

Berko believed him, happy Wolf-tattoo had not acknowledged the *nkisi* as the real culprit. The thief finally ceased his pacing and slumped in a chair, hyperventilating and looking a little glassy-eyed.

"I gotta get out of here. I don't wanna get fingered for this. I'm not going back in for an accident. I've got to sell what I can and disappear."

He didn't even bother trying to clean up Berko before tossing him back into the bag with the other stolen goods. The blood was fading as it dried anyway, indistinguishable from the stains Jojo's sacrifice had left behind.

The next thing Berko knew, he was moving again. He hoped the trip would offer him new opportunity for more *mpungo*, the younger the better.

❧❦

The pawnbroker, owner of the White Whale Odds and Ends, did not even bother to get a good look at Berko before offering a paltry lump sum for Wolf-tattoo's illegally acquired bounty. The thin Asian man who snapped out the price rather abruptly had dark circles under his eyes, the victim of a new baby who refused to sleep.

"That's it?" Wolf-tattoo asked. "Come on, man. I need money for the road. That won't get me far."

"I probably won't be able to sell half that junk. Take it or leave it," the vendor said with a yawn. He glanced from time to time up at the ceiling, a pained look on his tired face.

"Fine, whatever. I can't drag this around with me. I'll just have to stretch it out or figure something else along the way."

He begrudgingly took the money the pawnbroker held out and then, with a last frightened glance Berko's way, hurried out the door.

Without bothering to sort or shelve his newly obtained stock, the vendor dropped it all in the shop's backroom and returned to greet a customer at his counter.

The storeroom was nothing more than dust and shadows, quiet in all aspects but for the muffled sound carried back from the front of the shop. Berko lay amongst the small pile of ritual dolls and masks as the seconds ticked into minutes and then more than an hour, ever patient and waiting for change. Attentive in a way no human boy would be, his vigilance allowed him instant awareness of the faint sound that eventually trickled in from somewhere above.

The noise, a frail mewling, spurred Berko into a sitting position. He had enough magic in him at that point to move about much like a real boy could, even if he still could not speak, and his actions were somewhat stilted and awkward. All he needed was to make his way up to that glorious sound, one that pealed fresh *mpungo* ready for the taking, and he could fill up the empty spaces that plagued him.

Mine, he thought. Mine.

The young mother who slept above him, too exhausted to wake again at the first stirrings of her child, did not know the danger approaching from the depths of her family business. Nor did the baby whose cries were slowly increasing in volume, uncomfortable and fretful rather than afraid. The little one's father might have sensed something wrong, had he been less tired and distracted himself, but he was barely conscious enough to serve his customers.

As a result, there would be nobody coming to halt Berko's creeping progress up the stairs.

He moved onward and upward, licking his ochre lips.

❧❦

Jojo had been assessing the damage to his store when he heard the first of many shrill and plaintive screams. He had already noted Berko's disappearance along with other merchandise from his shop, realizing his worst fears had come to fruition. Despite his precautions, his *nkisi* had escaped, liberated by thieving vandals.

Knowing the *nkisi's* sole goal would be to fulfill its purpose and become the son Jojo had longed for, the *banganga* did not want to imagine what lengths the ritual doll might go to in order to reap the *mpungo* it still lacked. A prickly feeling in the pit of Jojo's stomach told him those screams would prove associated somehow with Berko's unplanned flight.

With this in mind, Jojo made his way toward the Asian quarter, the direction of the screams. He followed wordlessly along with a number of other people gathering to investigate the disturbance. He had not traveled far.

A hanging sign bearing a white whale marked the location of a pawnshop where he stopped, when a magical blue glow emanating from an alleyway caught his attention. Curious yet dreading what he would find, Jojo paused. He turned away from the small crowd and started off toward the source of the eerie illumination.

A few old crates and boxes cluttered the dead end of the alleyway, a place where local vendors discarded such things when they had no use for them. As Jojo got closer, the blue glow intensified, and he shied away, forced to shield his eyes. When the light dimmed enough and he could see again, Jojo gazed upon an unusual sight.

A boy Jojo guessed was perhaps eight or nine, stood at the very back of the alleyway among the crates, his dark skin, a reddish shade of brown, his mouth, an ochre hue, and his eyes the color of charcoal. Only a few wisps of coarse black hair covered the boy's head. He looked at Jojo and smiled, the expression somehow familiar to the *banganga*, even though the child appeared to be a stranger. That smile was all the more jarring in contrast to the horrible screams and exclamations of despair that continued to echo in from somewhere overhead.

Without trying, Jojo could sense the powerful magic flowing from the boy, released as his transformation came to an end. Like it or not, the *banganga* could not deny the mixture of *mpungo* dissipating included some of his own. It also contained spirit magic so fresh and powerful; it could have only come from one source. Jojo shuddered at the thought.

The boy seemed to be waiting for something, some acknowledgment. He stood staring at Jojo, dressed in tattered clothing stained with fresh blood that the old man was fairly certain was not his own. If this was Berko, that blood would have had to come from the ritual doll's last victim, before his change.

A sinking feeling plunged Jojo into unpleasant awareness, like immersion in ice-cold water. He took a step toward the placid boy, wondering if he had made a terrible mistake.

"Berko?"

The boy's eerie fleshy smile broadened. To answer Jojo's question, he reached into his mouth and pulled out the four *ovana* resting beneath his tongue. He extended them toward the *banganga*, his hand outstretched and palm upwards. Blood trickled from his sleeve, puddling on the pavement below his arm.

"Your wish has come true. The reaping of *mpungo* is complete. Your family legacy will live on in me."

Jojo recoiled, shaking his head. He realized his desire for a son by any means, blood of his blood, had inflicted unintentional tragedy upon another.

Jojo's efforts had brought about the loss of the truly innocent to sate the needs of his *nkisi*, a loss he had suffered once, too, and would never have wished upon anyone else.

"This isn't what I wished for at all. You are not my legacy. I have no family ties."

Berko laughed tossing the unclaimed *ovana* in Jojo's direction.

"Oh, but you do, Father, you do. Thanks to you, I'm a real boy now."

His laughter grew in volume to match the sobbing screams from above, a disturbing sight and discordant duet that would haunt the *banganga* for the rest of his wretched life.

Jojo tried walking away, but the quiet sound of small footsteps followed. There would be no escaping the cursed extension he had wrought upon his family. The boy he had spawned from evil was with him to stay.

No doubt, it would have been better to leave his family without ties and let his ancestral line die out peacefully. While he might have found a way to preserve it, at what cost had he done so?

The new family ties he had created were not just strings but shackles, manufactured from blood, *bakisi*, and death.

# COMMANDING THE STONES
*by Laurel Anne Hill*

Yana navigated the cobblestone street. Three times she almost twisted her ankle. Thank God the entrance to *Cimetière de Montmartre* lay just ahead. She turned. Her husband still lagged behind. Nikolay moved with the rapidity of a dying snail. Dammit. He had second thoughts about visiting Uncle Danilo's grave.

"You promised," she called to him. She'd need his help when climbing the steep stairs on the Parisian hillside.

"I can't go in there," Nikolay said as he approached her, his wide-eyed face pallid and strained. He looked like he'd bumped into his own ghost. "I thought I could, for you, but I can't."

What the heck would she do now? And how had Nikolay—owner of a funeral home in San Francisco—developed such a fear of cemeteries? But then, he'd changed since last Christmas. So had she.

"Besides," he added, "Peter's got business matters for me on the other side of town, a motivated seller."

"We wouldn't have any businesses if not for the money Uncle left me. Peter may be your cousin but Danilo was—"

"I know, I know." Nikolay fidgeted with a button on his leather coat. He ran his fingers through his gray-and-black hair. "Give Danilo my respects, all right? Listen, be thankful I haven't gone as crazy as he claimed his father was."

What a frigging lame comment. Still, the entrance to a graveyard was no place to blurt out the obscenities simmering within her. The best thing for her to do right then was feign calm.

"When will you get back to Peter's place?" Yana asked.

"I'm not sure." He clamped his narrow lips together. "Maybe eight o'clock."

He stepped backward—an avoidance maneuver, like Heaven and Hell forbade the demonstration of physical affection toward her.

"I'll have dinner ready."

She clenched her toes. Time to talk to the dead. Yana turned and ambled through the gateway. Where was the grounds guard? She didn't see any visitors, either, only a slate gray cat, like a shadow, lounging upon a granite slab.

Well, she couldn't depend on the cat for assistance. She'd have to climb those stairs by herself, even without a handrail, even if she had grown weak and thin since her last visit to Paris. Had only two years elapsed since 1995? Eight months since the onset of her heartburn hell? Yana sighed. Fifty-five was too young to teeter on the threshold of ghost-hood.

Ten minutes later, burning pains shot through Yana's legs. Her chest heaved ragged breaths. She'd climbed the cemetery staircase on her own—just barely.

Graves were squeezed together like passengers on the metro at rush hour. She stepped onto a patchwork of gravel and stone. Such a challenge, not to trip. Nikolay ought to have stayed with her. A real gentleman would have.

A real gentleman—ha! She sniffled. Nikolay wasn't even a real husband anymore. Why couldn't she have the old Nikolay back, the one who'd given her thirty-four years of joy? Clouds drifted through drab skies—a sad metaphor for her thirty-fifth year of marriage.

"So here I am," she muttered, "alone."

Except she wasn't alone. She knew the stained-glass window in that crypt's door. This elaborate stone angel, too. More weaving between graves brought Yana to a simple granite marker, flush with the ground. How good to behold the spot where Uncle rested.

Mid-afternoon shadows draped the familiar inscription.

*Danilo Yurkovich*
*1888-1963.*
*A man's greatest treasure is a worthy child.*

Dearest Danilo. He'd died and left her a million dollars when she was twenty-one. A million bucks! How? He'd been a dirt poor Russian immigrant who'd only owned two decent changes of clothes. His gift never ceased to amaze her. If her home had been in Paris instead of San Francisco, she would have visited his grave every day.

The chill of the November air brought a shiver. Yana buttoned the top of her bulky wool coat. She opened her handbag and withdrew the plastic sandwich bag holding Danilo's candy tin. Two Tootsie Rolls lay inside the dented container. She placed one on his grave stone.

"Would you like me to tell you our favorite story?" Yana smiled down at the granite. Her tear ducts stung.

"Once upon a time a thousand years ago—a master stone cutter and his son lived in the Ural Mountains. The boy stole an enchanted malachite flower from the Mistress of Copper Mountain. He refused to return it and soon died. Even the waters of life and death couldn't revive him."

The Stone Flower, Danilo's version of the fairy tale differed from all others. His certainly contained more violence and sadness. Tears rolled down Yana's cheeks, not because of the story, though.

"Uncle Danilo," she whispered between sobs, "my heart's heavy as your tombstone. All Nikolay cares about these days is finding stupid little antique boxes for Peter. He hasn't made love to me for a year, not even a kiss. I don't know what I've done wrong. You introduced us and always had such good advice. I wish you were still alive."

Yana blew her nose. If only life could be as simple as forty-nine years ago, when Danilo had told her Russian fairy tales and walked her up that San Francisco hill to grammar school.

She unwrapped the second Tootsie Roll and slid it into her mouth. How amazing the candy tasted, not like an ordinary Tootsie Roll. More like chocolate-and-butterscotch fudge. Well worth a case of indigestion. Danilo's little tin made magical improvements to cheap candy and always had.

A wind arose. Yana's chilly fingers numbed. She put on her fur-lined leather gloves and lowered her eyelids. If she concentrated hard, she could almost hear the irregular clumps of Danilo's work boots as he limped along a San Francisco sidewalk. She could almost smell the sweet smoky aroma from his pipe. On cold days such as this one, vapor would have puffed from between his stained front teeth and chapped lips.

"Russian magic," he'd always said when he'd given her one of his special Tootsie Rolls. "Don't tell your mother about what this box does. Never tell anyone."

"I won't," she'd promised.

❧❧

Four o'clock. Yana needed to leave the cemetery and shop for dinner. Tonight she'd cook for two. Peter was in Provence, searching for little ornate lacquer boxes.

Damn, she was tired of seeing little old lacquer boxes, although the men managed to make a good profit off most antiques and curiosities they acquired. What box could ever compare to Danilo's? Well, that treasure was her secret. She could never break a promise to her uncle.

Yana maneuvered between graves, then down the stairs. *Till death do us part.* Nikolay and she had promised each other so many things. As much as he exasperated her, she still loved him.

Perhaps she should prepare a special dinner tonight. Sardines sautéed in olive oil always pleased him. She would purchase chocolate from Angelina's, fresh bread from *Poilâne* Bakery, a fragrant cheese and a fine bottle of champagne. Who knew what might happen, other than her getting yet another case of heartburn? Maybe he would at least hold her hand.

A thumping sound came from behind her at the grassy roundabout. Rapid footsteps? Yana shifted to turn. A force slammed against her back. *Good God!* She toppled forward and landed on her hands and knees. Her shoulder purse dangled around her neck. Her empty canvas tote bag ended up somewhere else.

A man in dark clothing raced out through the gateway in front of her, like dragons breathed fire at his heels. Her stomach refluxed acid. Her hands and knees stung. A total of two people in the entire cemetery, and that guy had knocked her down.

A cat yowled and hissed. Yana stared in the direction of the noise. There was her tote bag. The slate gray kitty, back arched, stood on top. Uncle Danilo had always insisted cats brought good luck. Had the stupid stranger tried to steal her empty bag?

છ૭

Yana lugged her full tote bag and emerged from the metro near the left bank of the Seine. The shop lights beyond *Place Saint-Michel* filtered through a steady drizzle. Cold air stung her cheeks. Her nose dripped. The narrow streets smelled old, damp, and friendly.

She hadn't eaten much since breakfast and shouldn't try without Alka-Seltzer handy. Still, memories of sharing flaky croissants and *croques monsieur* with Nikolay in happier times awakened

172

her hunger. A man with bushy silver hair huddled under a striped awning, hands in the pockets of his brown leather jacket. Why, he stood by a pushcart, one with large bicycle wheels. Such an old cart—like something from a museum—and out of place in modern Paris.

"Would you like a *croque monsieur?*" the vendor asked in French, a broad-chested man in his late sixties with a double chin.

How had he known?

The man adjusted his wire-rimmed glasses, then lifted the square lid on the insulated cart. He withdrew two packages. She fumbled in her purse for money, smelling warm ham and melted cheeses.

"One is fine," she said. Her lack of an appropriate French accent marked her as a foreigner.

"Two are better, *Madame.*" He smiled, exposing several discolored front teeth, and then refused to accept money. "It's a cold night."

Two for free? She must have looked old and pathetic.

"Thank you, *Monsieur.* You're very kind."

She walked toward Peter's building, her shopping bag tugging at her forearm. The wrapped sandwiches she grasped smelled so good. Several clusters of pedestrians in bulky jackets or long coats wove around her. Like Yana, they avoided the narrow sidewalk. A car, the size of a golf cart, beeped and passed. She stopped and devoured one entire sandwich, her lips buttery and warm. So much food at once, the way she used to eat before Nikolay's feelings for her had changed.

The smell of fresh oranges grew strong, as if Uncle Danilo peeled and sectioned fruit in front of her nose. Next came the wonderful odor of peanut butter. Danilo had always made her school lunch sandwiches extra thick. And, oh, when he'd packed a cabbage roll stuffed with rice and lamb. Yana's shoulders sagged. Danilo. Nikolay. Good food that had never upset her stomach. She drowned in her own lost past.

Yana punched in a security code and entered the enclosed cobblestone courtyard of the seventeenth-century building. She groped for the light switch. A row of dented garbage cans lined the brick wall of an alcove. A gray cat raced out from behind one. A stalker could crouch back there and she'd never know. That stranger in the cemetery. Her heart beat faster. With one hand on the railing, she ascended the spirals of a wooden staircase to a tiled landing on the third floor, Peter's door.

An emerald glow bathed the wood, then vanished. Yana blinked and tightened her grip on Peter's key. She was tired. Her imagination worked overtime.

❧❧

Nikolay's fork made a soft clatter as he set it on his china dinner plate. A morsel of sautéed sardine flipped from the fork to the ivory linen tablecloth, producing an oily stain.

"Some stranger knocked you down in the cemetery?" He gripped the crystal stem of his champagne flute. "You should have told me sooner."

"No real damage done. Just a couple scrapes and bruises." At least Nikolay appeared concerned for her and had since he'd returned here tonight. Yana smiled. "I figured the story could wait."

"Damn!" His cheeks reddened. "A maniac's running around that part of town. Didn't you tune in to the evening news?"

"No, I—"

"An old woman's been murdered," Nikolay said. "For a few pieces of costume jewelry. In Montmartre. That could have been you."

"Merciful God." Yana stared down at the glistening diamonds in her wedding ring. Perhaps wearing gloves had saved her.

"Did he try to steal anything from you?" Nikolay said.

"I don't think so. My purse strap was around my neck. I dropped my shopping bag, but it was empty then."

Except for yesterday's receipts. Had any of those receipts included her credit card number? How careless to have left them in the side pocket of her tote bag. Yana hurried from the dinner table to the coat hooks in the entryway. She dug her hand into the bag's pocket. Plenty of receipts remained in there, including the ones she sought.

The bag's side pocket contained something else. She withdrew a piece of jewelry, a pin. Where had it come from? She turned the pin right side up and gasped. Malachite, shaped like a rose, a stone flower just like in the fairy tale she'd recited beside Uncle Danilo's grave.

The tick of Peter's cuckoo clock resonated in the hallway. The carved wooden bird did its thing. *A bird...a cat.* The slate gray cat had stood on her bag in the cemetery and hissed.

"Nikolay," she called. "Did the news report describe the stolen property?"

"Not really," he said. "Oh, one piece might have been malachite. No gold or expensive gems."

"Oh, then we have a problem." Yana's stomach roiled. She carried the brooch to the dinner table. "That man left me a gift."

She set the brooch on the tablecloth. Nikolay just sat there, his eyes wider than a full-open door. He scratched the side of his Roman nose. Then he picked up the brooch and turned it over in the palm of his hand.

"Shit," he said.

"We'd better call the police." So much for her plans of holding hands after dinner.

"No," Nikolay said, his voice firm. "Not yet."

"Then when?" Yana's face flushed warm. This was serious. Why did he have to protest her advice?

"Peter has to see this brooch." He pointed to the tiny curly-cue mark on the pin's back. "It's a special one."

Special jewelry as well as special boxes?

"It's special all right," Yana said. "The rightful owner died because of it."

"She wasn't the rightful owner."

Not the true owner? How would Nikolay know? And why had that man—that murderer—who'd knocked Yana down in the cemetery, put the brooch in her bag? *Oh, dear God.* She stared at the pin, then at her husband.

"What do you know about this brooch?" Yana whispered. "About the death of that poor woman?"

"For crying out loud," Nikolay said, "don't look at me that way. I didn't kill her, and I don't know who did. I think Peter's the pin's rightful owner, though. When he was a kid, that woman's husband may have cheated his father out of it."

"Peter?"

"He's been trying to buy a brooch back ever since some woman's husband died ten years ago. His description of the piece matches this. It belonged to his great-grandfather."

Nikolay pushed back from the table and stood. He closed the maroon velvet drapes in the living room, and then eased the table and chairs clear of the window area.

"You getting the pin was more than a coincidence," Nikolay said. "That man must have put this building under surveillance, seen us and Peter all together. He probably committed the murder sometime before dawn, then came here and followed us to the cemetery."

"But, why?"

"I've no idea, but we're in danger. We need to fly back to San Francisco as soon as possible. I'll put the brooch in the drawer where Peter keeps his revolver. We'll call him from the airport and let him know what's happened."

"Oh, Nikolay," Yana said. "I'm scared."

"So am I." He returned to the table. "Yana, I never should have left you at the cemetery alone.

Peter has besieged me with crazy schemes since last Christmas. My head's existed in places that don't exist." He stepped even closer to her. His fingers tilted her chin upward. "Today I felt too ashamed of myself to even stand in front of Danilo's grave. Can you ever forgive me?"

"I love you." She read the softness in his dark eyes. Of course she forgave him.

He bent over her and kissed her forehead, then her lips. His warm hands clasped hers and gave them a squeeze. This was the first time he'd shown real affection toward her in so long. Nikolay was her husband again.

"I'll throw our important things into a suitcase." The expression on his face reflected more relief than fear. "You dig out the airline tickets and call a cab."

Yana nodded. Nikolay let go of her hands. He picked up the brooch and pivoted in the direction of Peter's bedroom. Green light flashed from the pin. His foot slipped. He clutched his chest. The pin fell from his grasp. He staggered and groaned.

"Nikolay!" Yana sprang up from her seat. His sturdy frame thudded against the carpeted floor. Had he drunk too much champagne?

"Nikolay." Yana reached him and sank to her knees. "My love!"

She clung to his broad shoulders, tried to shake him. Why didn't he respond? Almighty Father, Nikolay wasn't breathing. CPR...phone for help. What should she do first? But she couldn't move.

The light from the brass floor lamp flickered and went out. A sea-green luminescence oozed toward her in the semi-darkened room, like phosphorescent fog creeping into a harbor. It smelled of dampness and decay. Of evil, too? She had to shield Nikolay. Somehow her body inched its way on top of him. She prayed in English, French, and Russian. The mist flowed over them both.

He and the green vapor vanished. She dropped against the carpet. Gone! Nikolay was gone. Like in some crazy magic show. He'd been there, underneath her on the rug. She couldn't have imagined him. Terror blazed through Yana like jolts of electricity.

"Give him back!" Yana shouted.

"*Then return the stone flower to where it belongs*," a feminine voice replied in Russian. "*And, please, not to Peter. Peter, he is not the rightful owner.*"

Who'd said that? Yana shifted sideways, her hip and elbow pressed against the rug. Her glance darted sixteen feet upward to the loft, then shot to the storage cabinet behind an overstuffed chair. The door appeared closed. She had to be alone. Had to be.

A soft, plunking sound emanated from an indiscernible location—dripping water. Yana tensed her hands against the raised pile of the Chinese carpet. All the remaining lights in the room went out.

Yana groped near the fireplace for a flashlight. The plunking sound intensified behind her. She turned. An emerald flash stabbed her eyes.

Dark spots danced in the air. Maybe she could crawl toward Peter's phone and get help.

*"A man's greatest treasure is a worthy child,"* the voice said.

"Treasure rewards worthiness," Yana whispered in English. Danilo had written that in a note to her when he'd gone back to live in France. A year later he'd died and bequeathed her his fortune.

*"Want to know what to do?"* the voice asked. Surely the Mistress of Copper Mountain spoke. *"Command the stones and find out."*

Lamplight swelled and illuminated the living room. The brooch no longer glowed. Coarse green dust, like ground malachite, lay on the carpet where Nikolay had collapsed. A little of the dust clung to Yana.

Her eyes streamed tears. Her nose clogged. She needed Kleenex and retrieved her purse from the couch. Folded tissues sat inside the plastic bag containing Danilo's box.

The dented surface of the tin warmed her hand. She cast a nervous glance toward the stone flower and examined the box. A faint arabesque she'd never noticed gleamed on the lid. This was like one of Peter and Nikolay's special boxes.

Her throat tightened, as if two hands cut off her air. The walls spun, a flurry of silvers and greens. The malachite brooch and antique boxes. The old woman's murder. Nikolay's death and disappearance. All were pieces of a puzzle awaiting connection.

If Yana needed to command the stones, first she'd better calm down and think. To think, she'd better eat. She'd barely touched her dinner. She prepared a cup of peppermint tea. Instead of eating a sardine, she nibbled on the second toasted sandwich from the street vendor.

Both the brooch and box possessed magical powers. Both had that curly-cue mark. Peter had searched for special boxes and wanted the pin back. He had to be seeking powers for himself. A thief had strangled an old woman for the pin. Yana had once seen Peter smash his fist through a door. Peter might know the thief...be the thief, but who'd delivered the pin to Yana? And why?

Had Nikolay been involved? He'd proclaimed his innocence. He couldn't have participated in murder. She'd known him so well. Or, had she? She coughed hard. Why hadn't he let her notify the police?

The Mistress of Copper Mountain. Yana pictured a stone sorceress with green skin—hair threaded with thousands of pinpoint emeralds and flecks of polished onyx—the owner of a magical garden of carved malachite roses. Return the stone flower to get Nikolay back. Danilo's harmless fairy tale had become Yana's deadly reality.

❧❦

A special pin belonged in a special box. The combination belonged in a safe place—Yana's money belt. Too bad the stone flower's light blazed through the box, belt, and her sweater. She looked like a walking lantern.

Black absorbed light, didn't it? She put on her black wool coat and hoped for the best.

Peter's revolver—he kept the gun in his night stand or on him. She raced to his bedroom. His pistol was gone. Not good.

She circled the living room, and then peered between the draperies and out the window. No thuds of footsteps on the stairs. If Peter wanted her dead, where could she seek safety? The American Consulate was closed. The police would hear her story and pronounce her insane.

"Is commanding the stones like making a wish?" She glanced down toward her money belt. "What do I ask for?"

How weird to expect an answer from a box and a pin. Yana crossed her arms against her chest and rubbed her shoulders. Would she gain magical powers by commanding the stones? She didn't want power. She wanted Nikolay back.

*"It won't work if I reveal too many details,"* the Mistress of Copper Mountain said. She didn't show herself. *"Try harder."*

"I already am."

The lamplight flickered. Pain blazed up Yana's arm and down her spine. She fought for breath. She needed a source of strength—a prayer, a memory of Nikolay.

The pain stopped. Yana sucked in air, her gasps short and shallow. Another onslaught could kill her. Plunks of dripping water drummed like impatient fingers.

"Flag of truce," Yana said. "I'll try harder."

She pressed her hands against her money belt and stomach. A bizarre magical entity expected her to issue an ingenious directive. Still, a comforting feeling enveloped her, like the warmth of Nikolay's arms. Maybe she didn't need to understand all of this.

"You want me to return you someplace," Yana said. "And Peter wants you for himself." She shook her head from side to side. The answer was so clear. "I command you to do what's best."

Emerald mist spiraled from between the buttons on her coat. Yana smelled peanut butter, chocolate-butterscotch fudge, and pastries stuffed with cabbage and lamb. Russian magic approved of her decision. Maybe Uncle Danilo did, too.

"*You and me*," the Mistress of Copper Mountain said, "*we cut across the Seine, go beyond the Arc de Triomphe to the church of Saint Alexandre Nevsky.*"

"Why there?"

The Mistress of Copper Mountain didn't answer. Maybe only a Russian Orthodox priest could deal with unorthodox Russian magic.

❧

It was one in the morning on Saturday. The metro was closed and taxis scarce. The distance between Peter's flat and the church of Saint Alexandre Nevsky would not concern a young woman. Yana's legs, however, might give out before she even reached the Seine.

She found Peter's penlight, and then retied the laces on her boots. The homeless often slept in a tunnel near the river's quay. Less of a threat than Peter, if he'd returned to Paris.

Yana descended the staircase to the courtyard. Icy rain sprinkled her cheeks and nose.

Snow could fall before sunrise. She lifted the hood of her coat. The street outside appeared deserted. Best to stay close to buildings, despite dog droppings on the sidewalks.

At the end of the first block, she listened for the slosh of galoshes against wet pavement, for a cough—any evidence of being followed. Peter sometimes wore Nikes in rainy weather. She glanced behind her. Nobody there.

She cut down a narrow, unlit street. Her fleece-lined boots clicked with each step. How far away could her footsteps be heard? She quickened her pace, surprised by the relative ease of walking. Did magic provide strength? Or did fear?

Cold air and persistent congestion irritated her lungs. She fought the impulse to cough and pinpoint her location. By then, Peter might have surmised she still had the brooch. God, was he really her enemy? He was a cousin and business partner. She'd cooked him so many meals.

Yana passed an open manhole, its metal barricade in place. Only a dolt would have left a sewer entry port open at this hour. A soft clink of metal behind her made her flinch. She ducked into an alley and flattened herself against a building, her heart hammering hard.

A figure passed by on the main street, its pace brisk. Over six feet tall—a man. She waited, taking quiet little breaths. It could be Peter or his hired thug—or simply an errant husband headed home from a tryst. Peter wouldn't shoot her in front of others. She should hide until Paris awakened. She could pound on the door of a bakery. No, there wasn't one nearby.

A cat meowed. The slate gray kitty sat beside the open manhole. More plunks of dripping water resonated. Yana patted her coat. Both cat and brooch prompted her to seek refuge in the sewer system? She couldn't hide in there—not with roaches, muck, and rats. And cleaners would wash the streets at dawn. Between rain and runoff, she'd drown.

She recalled the way Peter clenched his jaws when angry. He weighed two hundred-ten pounds, was only fifty and fit as hell. Her stomach churned.

☙❧

Yana descended a metal ladder inside the manhole, groping for holds. The air smelled damp with a hint of rotten eggs. It coated her tongue with a foul taste. The heel of her boot snagged the hem of her long coat. Her foot reached through several inches of water and made contact with the floor of the cavern.

A soft, scampering sound tensed her muscles. Rats. Yana moved away from the ladder, edging sideways along the wall. She had to maintain a sense of direction. Otherwise, she'd never find her way out. Something scurried under her gloved hands. Roaches! She jerked her hands and shook them. No matter what happened, she mustn't scream.

She advanced several yards into the blackness, her fingertips brushing the sewer wall. The wall curved, a junction with another passage.

A metallic clatter led to a thud. Yana froze in position. Someone must have entered the sewer. A pool of yellow light stretched along the opposite wall. A bevy of roaches scattered.

"I know you're down here," Peter said.

Peter was involved. She hadn't wanted to believe it. Truth showed itself, and he'd found her so soon.

Panic wouldn't help. Yana maneuvered around the curve of the wall. She crouched in the runoff, praying the beam would miss her. Moisture seeped through her clothing. Her leg muscles threatened to cramp. The dank atmosphere scratched at her lungs. How could she keep from coughing?

"I've been following you," Peter said. He sounded closer. "Did you really think you could hide?"

Irregular sloshes of water heralded Peter's advance. Yana's lungs ached. Her chest heaved in violent, uncontrollable spasms. The beam from a flashlight stabbed her eyes. Hacking, she groped the stone wall. She had to escape.

"You've ruined your pretty coat," Peter said. "What a shame." He cleared his throat with a single guttural rasp. "Where's Nikolay? He was supposed to be at the cemetery this afternoon." His menacing voice echoed.

"I don't have the faintest notion where Nikolay is," Yana said. "We had an argument."

"A tiff over a pin, perhaps?"

Peter knew about the brooch. The broad beam from his flashlight wobbled. Yana's eyes adjusted to the harsh illumination. Only Nikolay had known of her plan to visit the graveyard. He and Peter were partners in crime, after all. Dear

Lord, she'd put herself in this position to save Nikolay, and here she was, as helpless as a mouse bracing for a cobra's strike.

"My dear cousin didn't want you or that old woman harmed," Peter said, his voice flat. "Things happen."

Peter sloshed toward Yana. She could see his face, his pinched, angry expression. He towered over her, his pant legs and the lower hem of his trench coat drenched. Nikolay had planned to leave the pin behind for Peter. If he hadn't wanted anyone harmed, why had the Mistress of Copper Mountain struck him down? Because he'd decided to relinquish the stone flower to Peter?

"Give me the brooch," Peter said. His light probed her cowering form. "Don't try anything foolish."

Yana slid her hands into the dark water. Cold liquid oozed down her gloves. She pushed against the sewer floor to stand. That foul smell grew.

Peter had no intention of letting her live. He didn't want to search her dead body in the muck, that's all. At least Nikolay—wherever he was—remained beyond his cousin's reach. If she kept a clear head, an opportunity to escape and save him might arise. The stone flower had to reach the Church of Alexandre Nevsky.

"I don't understand." She had to buy time to devise a plan. "We were going to give you the pin."

Yana studied his tight grip on the flashlight. Could she get away if he dropped the light in the water? It might leak or break.

"Just hand me the brooch," he said.

The sound of dripping water returned. A product of magic or rain? Peter slid his hand into the pocket of his trench coat. His gun must be there. How far would the sound of shots carry? Not far, if he had a silencer. Perhaps Peter would miss. She would pretend to be dead. Help might come. No, Peter wouldn't miss.

"I deserve to know what this is all about," Yana said.

Peter shrugged. "Why not?" He sloshed backward, as if wary of her schemes.

"My great-grandfather fled from Russia to Paris before the Bolshevik uprising," he said. "He got his family out, as you know, much of his vast fortune, too." Peter spat into the water. "He was a crazy, mean-spirited bastard and couldn't die soon enough, as far as his children were concerned."

The dripping intensified. Peter didn't appear to notice. The stone flower tried to deliver another cryptic message.

"Great-Grandpa dabbled in magic, not with enough cunning. He lost to the devil." Peter's voice—the rhythm of water trickling over stones varied as he spoke.

"Each of the old man's children inherited a paltry sum," Peter said. "Each received a lacquer box, a malachite brooch, and a letter from him. According to his letter, one of the pins and one of the boxes were enchanted."

Watery gurgles echoed, accentuating Peter's speech. "Any person who placed the magic pin inside the magic box would receive Great-Grandpa's magical powers and greatest treasure." Peter sneered. "The wretch was worth millions.

You can imagine the inevitable consequences. No matter. I've got all ten boxes now, and you have the right pin."

The pin. Ten boxes. His great-grandpa's greatest treasure. Yana's mind reeled. What hidden key lay within those words? Danilo's box had a curly-cue scratch. Both box and stones did magic without each other.

Peter drew his gun. Blood pounded through Yana's temples. She was going to die, but she hadn't yet rescued Nikolay.

Maybe the sewer led to Alexander Nevsky's. If she tossed the brooch into the water, a current could wash it in the proper direction. She needed to have faith. A priest would exorcise the magic. Peter would never possess the power of the stones. She had to keep him talking.

"Time's up," Peter said. "The pin. Give it to me now."

No more time... Yana fumbled with the buttons on her coat. How far could she throw the brooch? Her frail hands felt huge and clumsy. A feminine voice inside of her head called her name.

"*A man's greatest treasure is a worthy child*," the Mistress of Copper Mountain said. "*Count the drops of water.*"

Yana stood transfixed. Eleven drops plunked. Not ten, not the same as the number of boxes Peter had mentioned. She burped up bile. Danilo. His screwed-up Russian father. Her inheritance. The candy tin. Peter's great-grandfather had never meant anyone to put the right pin into the right box, win his magical powers and a big prize. He'd handed out the prize first— to his most cherished son. The rest had followed.

Peter straightened his gun arm. Yana sloshed toward him. The thug in dark clothing had given her the pin. The Mistress of Copper Mountain must have frightened him in the cemetery.

Peter fired, and then fired again. Danilo had given her his box. The Mistress of Copper Mountain was on Yana's side. Didn't Peter realize he couldn't hurt her? A rushing sound stabbed her eardrums.

"Your great-grandpa owned an eleventh box," she shouted. "He bequeathed it to his illegitimate son."

An ebony wall of water swelled from nowhere. The wave towered behind Peter and crashed over them both. Yana snapped shut her eyes and held her breath. Peter cursed.

A force hurled her against the sewer wall. Phosphorescent faces undulated in swirls of putrid foam. Yana could see them with her eyes closed. Maggots squirmed from between countless pairs of ugly, twisted lips. Yana opened her eyes. A malachite woman—ruby eyed with claw fingers— enveloped Peter. The Mistress of Copper Mountain clutched her prey. Cascades of water ran crimson—turned into blood.

Peter screamed. Yana vomited.

❧

Yana stood, wet and shivering, pressed against the sewer wall. A yellow beam shone through the murky water where Peter's flashlight lay. The blood and mystical woman had vanished. Peter was gone, too. Yana patted her money belt, her hand trembling. Danilo's box and the brooch were there. Safe. The Mistress of Copper Mountain still wanted her to take the pin to the church.

"Does anybody need help?" a male voice called in French.

Someone must have heard Peter's gunshots or scream. A faint shaft of light penetrated the darkness, twenty or thirty feet away. Yana called out and sloshed toward it with the dripping flashlight. The two beams intersected. She climbed the ladder, her legs unsteady. A strong hand gripped her wrist and pulled. She grunted. How wonderful to fill her lungs with fresh air. She looked upward.

"*Madame?*" the sandwich vendor said, his lips parted and eyes wide. The moon gleamed beyond his shoulder.

What was he doing here? Yana thanked him, without smiling. He obviously questioned her sanity. She saw little point in grinning like a total fool.

"I've always wanted to explore a sewer," she said and straightened her sopping coat. At least she hadn't spewed the garment with vomit.

"Are you walking far?" the man asked. He removed his gloves and lit a cigarette.

"Past the *Arc de Triomphe*."

"It's on my way." He exhaled smoke into the icy air.

He moved in step with her. Yana's soggy boots sloshed. She was weary and glad to have company. The man's nose was flat, not at all like

Nikolay's. Nikolay. He'd vanished. Peter had vanished. The cigarette smoke smelled pungent and good.

"Earlier, when I gave you the sandwiches, I was minding a stranger's cart," the man said. "You reminded me of someone I once knew." He took a long drag on his cigarette. "You are not she, of course."

The cold penetrated Yana's wet clothing. Her spine and legs ached. Did the man speak of a former mistress? A wife who'd died? She glanced around. How strange to see no parked cars. And the street had cobblestones instead of regular pavement. She didn't know this part of Paris as well as she'd thought.

"Would you like a Tootsie Roll?" The man adjusted his glasses and extracted a small metal tin from his coat pocket.

The tin looked like the one in Yana's money belt. She didn't know a lot of things as well as she'd thought.

He placed the candy on her tongue. Chocolate and butterscotch fudge melted together. She half-closed her eyes, the candy wedged against the inner surface of her cheek.

"I've a modest flat," the man said, without turning toward her. "The water usually runs." He lit another cigarette. "It's near Alexandre Nevsky."

The sandwich man lived near the church? Threads of fate connected this strangeness to the stone flower. She stumbled. The man gripped her arm.

"Please forgive me," Yana said. Her soiled coat brushed his. "It's been an unusual night."

"My jacket is old, nothing to worry about." He clasped her arm tighter. The rhythm of his galoshes on the pavement was uneven, as if he limped. "I've had an odd night, too. You're the second person who's needed my help."

The second person? Yana smelled peanut butter and pipe tobacco. Who was this guy? And who was the person he'd helped?

"Did you hurt your leg tonight?" she said.

"No."

Yana had expected that answer. Something was both right and wrong. She glanced down a street. Hadn't a neon light once flashed above that pharmacy? And where was her favorite little café? She lowered her eyelids and took a deep breath.

"And, where, may I ask is that other person now?"

"Sleeping in my flat. He just turned up on my doorstep. Appeared out of nowhere with a cat. Both covered in dust, gritty and green."

Coarse, green dust? Like in Peter's flat? And that cat again. Yana exhaled with a whistle. The brooch had never needed to go all the way to the church.

"My mother used to tell me cats bring good luck." He laughed. "It's good that poor fellow found one."

"Yes," Yana whispered.

Once upon a time a discouraged woman had prayed beside her uncle's grave. The waters of life and death had revived her body and soul, brought her to a strange yet familiar place. Whatever happened—or didn't—between her and the green dust man would be all right. Even if he looked nothing like Nikolay anymore.

Christmas tea spiced with cloves would taste nice at breakfast. The sandwich man would find an open bakery. Bring home a bag of croissants, custard squares, and raisin rolls. She would prepare omelets. He would section fresh oranges. The green dust man would awaken in time to eat. They all would discuss many things. Indigestion wouldn't be one of them.

"I've a remarkable piece of jewelry," Yana said. The magic was for her now. She could safely confide. "Perhaps you'll recognize the pin and its special little jewelry box. Perhaps not." If he didn't, the cat would. "I feel I've owned them for a thousand years."

# GOLLEWON ELLEE
*by DJ Tyrer*

It was a glorious summer about ten years since the Queen had died and not long after her son had come to the throne. Such events seemed far from the Mount but were drilled into the minds of Liza Cardle and her classmates nonetheless. Now the end of term was at hand and with it freedom from the drudgery and confinement of the stuffy classroom. The summer might have meant hard work in the fields, but she relished that in comparison to struggling with her lessons. The letters and numbers she was supposed to master seemed to dance about on the page before her, resistant to all her attempts to make sense of them. Her failure more often than not resulted in the application of the cane to her palm. The calluses earned from hard work were far preferable to the shameful and stinging marks of punishment.

As much as the summer meant work, it also meant liberty. Even with the abandonment of the western half of the village that had lain beyond the church and the transformation of the land into a field, there were still plenty of people to do all the necessary farm work that dominated the summer months. The children were not expected to labor all the time, but were allowed to wander as they would on occasion if all their necessary duties had been fulfilled. Unlike the set hours of the school day, there was ample time for fun.

The village lay beside the road running east-to-west across the hill, north of the Common. Liza lived in a small brick-built cottage unpleasantly close, in her opinion, to the schoolhouse. She would much prefer to live on the west side of the village in the shadow of the great stone church with its austere beauty, as did her friend, Mairee Mago.

Where Liza was slight and pale with long golden locks, Mairee was rather stout with dark hair and the ruddy cheeks of healthy country folk. Even when she spent her days out in the fields in the sun, Liza never quite darkened. Her mother always said her slim build and ankles were sure indicators of gentle blood running in their veins, not that having gentle blood in one's veins offered any benefits she could see. Besides, Mairee's name was supposed to indicate descent from the lordly line as certainly as any Dawson or Harleyson, and *her* ankles were anything but slim.

It was Mairee who told Liza she had seen lights in Monastery Woods.

"I saw them from my bedroom window," she told her. "*Gollewon Ellee*." Fairy Lights.

"What were they doing?"

"I don't know, just moving about amongst the trees. It's too far away to see clearly, and the church is sort of in the way."

Liza was uncertain whether to take Mairee at her word. Enigmatic lights were more plausible than some of the things she claimed to have seen, so Liza thought it was quite likely she had seen them.

"When did you see them?" Liza asked.

"I think it was about an hour after midnight."

"We should go into the woods and look for them."

Mairee agreed, and they arranged to meet outside her house at midnight in order to explore the woods. Thus neither had any particular concerns, just fascination and anticipation.

Liza felt a real sense of excitement as she waited for the sun to go down and wished it were not one of the long days of summer. Her mother seemed surprised at her sudden willingness to go to bed without argument, but appeared to accept repeated nagging had finally produced results.

Once abed, Liza found it difficult to sleep, desperate for midnight to come. She knew she ought to sleep to pass the time and refresh herself for the adventure ahead, but was worried she would not wake on time. With a certain inevitability, sleep crept up on her shortly before the specified hour, and she very nearly missed their meeting.

"You're late," Mairee stated when Liza joined her a short distance from her house.

"Sorry." She yawned widely.

Somewhere in the woods beyond the fields an owl hooted, answered by another further away. The owls, the nocturnal stand-ins for the ravens, were ubiquitous to the Mount, and their cries could regularly be heard if you remained awake past the setting of the sun.

"Right, let's go," Mairee said, taking Liza's hand and pulling the yawning girl after her.

"No need to rush, just give me a chance to wake up!"

The Monastery Woods lay on the western slope of the hill. A couple of miles in that direction, hidden amongst the dense woodland, laid the village of Crayk and the ill-omened hamlet of Kill Gorakh. They wouldn't be going that far, just down the slope a little way. The lights Mairee said she'd seen had only been a little way into the woods, and Liza had a theory as to where they might be headed.

To reach the woods, they had to cross the road and enter Old Oak Field next to the paddock and then over a stile into Fox Field.

"We ought to find some place to hide," she suggested as they walked through the high-stalked wheat. "Somewhere from which we can watch for the *Gollewon Ellee*."

"How about over in the corner of the field there?" She pointed with the light of the half-moon enough to reveal the silhouette of the hedge. "It's pretty overgrown, but there's a gap there where we can lay down and watch."

"Easier said than done," Liza said after several minutes of searching. The heavy growth meant it was deep in shadow and hard to see. Still, it did mean they would be well concealed.

"Here it is. Watch out, it's thorny." They slithered their way beneath the arched branches of the bushes, thorns tugging at their clothes. Thankfully, the long, hot days of summer meant the ground was baked solid so there was no mud, not even much dusty soil, to dirty their clothing and risk parental displeasure.

The gap, a short tunnel through the foliage crafted by some nocturnal creature, was large enough for them to lie close together and stare out at the darkness beneath the trees abutting the field. Even with the moonlight, little was visible in the woods. For the first time that night, Liza felt a little nervous. From the way Mairee shivered beside her, she guessed her friend, too, was feeling a frisson of fear at the deep darkness. Even here in the early hours, the night was far too warm for the involuntary movement to be caused by cold. She groped for Mairee's hand and gave it a reassuring squeeze as they waited. Her friend returned the pressure, and she felt a little braver.

"Something's sticking into me," Mairee commented after a few minutes, wriggling to try and get comfortable.

Liza hoped they would see the lights soon, although they had not been waiting long. She wished she could be certain Mairee hadn't been making them up. Even if the lights were real, it was entirely possible it was just someone hunting rabbits or something equally mundane.

Only the hardness of the ground stopped her from drifting off into sleep.

Suddenly, Mairee let out a little noise of excitement. Liza's eyes snapped open, and she looked at the woods.

"The lights."

There was a procession of maybe a dozen bluish-white lights bobbing along amongst the trees. If Liza had to guess, she'd say they were coming down the hill, carefully picking their way down the slope. There were stories of such mysterious lights amongst the ruins of the castle and the long-abandoned Harley house atop the hill.

The lights would sometimes proceed down the hill on whatever strange business fairies or ghosts might have. It seemed unlikely they had come from the very peak of the hill—they surely would have descended at a point nearer to the top—but then, who knew what reasoning such things might follow?

She had a suspicion the procession was headed toward the avenue of stones hidden amongst the trees. They were not far from the 'Eye of the Needle', the single stone at the southern end of the avenue. The far end of the avenue culminated at a barrow that some said was a gateway to the city of the Fair Folk. Was that where the lights were headed, the lanterns, perhaps, of a band of the Fey traveling from one hidden abode to another?

"Can you see who they are?" Mairee asked, a tremble of fear in her voice.

It was difficult to say whether they truly wished their curiosity to be satisfied. There were stories of travelers encountering visions of those doomed to die within the year and of the risen dead said to stalk the hill through the hours of darkness in search of the blood of the living.

"I thought I saw somebody, but there are trees in the way. You can only really see the glow of the lights, nothing more."

"We need to move closer." Mairee's voice indicated she would rather not pursue her own suggestion.

"They aren't very far away." If they waited much longer, though, they would be. The last of the lights was parallel with the girls' position and about to head away from them. She half wanted to turn and head back to her comfortable bed, but curiosity was proving too strong a lure. "Oh, come on."

Slowly and carefully, the girls crawled out from under the hedge and crouching low began to follow the bluish glow of the *Gollewon Ellee* as they threaded their way between the trees.

The canopy of the trees was thick and filtered the moon glow to the merest trace. The lights they were following were too far away and screened by the trees to act as anything other than a guide to the direction they should follow. At most, they could make out the trunks of the trees and the thicker of their roots and branches. Unfortunately, it was not bright enough to discern the others, less obvious obstacles lining their path. They had to pick their way carefully, groping as if they were playing Blind Man's Bluff.

Mairee let out a yelp of mixed pain and fear as something thorny caught at her leg.

"Oh! I thought it was a claw!" she exclaimed as she dabbed at the blood it had drawn.

"Shush!" hissed Liza. "They mustn't hear us." She didn't need to elaborate the various harms said to befall those who spied upon the Fair Folk such as blindness, lameness, confusion, madness, even outright disappearance.

Not quite taking the hint, Mairee stopped to say, "Something clawed my leg, actually, and it hurt!" Her voice was shriller than it ought to have been, and Liza winced at the sound.

"Shush!"

A loud hoot above made them both jump, giving involuntary shrieks. Looking up, they watched as an owl detached itself from the trunk of a tree and perched on a branch above their heads, gazing down at them with enormous black eyes like pits in a pale, colorless circle of a face. It hooted again and continued to stare. Liza shivered. It was almost as if the owl was sounding an alert to her presence. She knew geese could be good guardians and wondered if the owls served the Fair Folk in such a capacity. They were supposed to have their own hounds, hunting hounds said to run with the legendary hunt and seize the souls of sinners. Did the owls supplement them in their role as guard dogs for their dwellings beneath the hill? If not, the owl was being very inconvenient.

The owl slipped back into the shadow of the trunk, vanishing as if it had never been there. There was no sign that those they followed had been alerted by the sound. The lights continued to move away down the hill.

"Hurry up!" she hissed at Mairee. If they dawdled any longer they were certain to lose the procession.

They made their way down the slope as swiftly as they could in the shadows. The ground began to level out. The slopes of the Mount did not descend smoothly but were almost stepped, as if shaped by the actions of man rather than nature. Liza knew the avenue of standing stones ran along the area of level ground. As she had guessed, it seemed as if the lights were proceeding along the course of the avenue.

Another owl hooted and flew between the trees ahead of them.

"I'm scared, Liza..."

"Me, too. Maybe we should–"

She didn't have the chance to finish her sentence as a figure stepped out of the shadows before them. The figure had two arms, two legs, and a head, but it wasn't human. Although they could not see it clearly, there was something about it that made the two girls certain of that fact. In the darkness, it was colorless, a shadow amongst deeper shadows. All they could see with any clarity was a pair of large black eyes like pits staring unblinkingly at them as it barred their way.

For a moment, all was silent and still, then Mairee let out a piercing shriek of purest terror, turned, and ran. Driven solely by fright, she ran heedlessly between the trees and vanished within moments from Liza's sight. Liza had turned, automatically, to follow her friend's sudden movement, but remained still. Liza was too startled to really do anything at all.

Although she could barely see the figure—it was almost a shadow given depth—Liza knew it wasn't human. No human being could have eyes that large and deep. They looked more like the sockets of a skull than real eyes, yet seemed to bore deep within her as if looking into her soul. It was as if she were beyond fear or outside of herself, watching the scene from somewhere else. It was a strange sensation she had never felt before.

The figure stepped toward her. She flinched. It was like an oversized baby in outline, her height, with a huge head and spindly limbs. At a closer proximity, she guessed it was pale like a corpse, although it was impossible to really tell in the darkness. A feeling of menace flowed almost tangibly from it to her.

"You shouldn't have come here," said a voice somewhere to her left, putting into words the feeling within her. It was a peculiarly sweet voice melodious, like a child's. The very innocence of the voice made her feel uneasy. Such sweetness of voice did not necessarily betoken a sweetness of disposition or motivation. Liza remembered someone saying the Devil could appear as an angel of light, not just as a dark and monstrous being portrayed by the statue the eccentric priest erected in the church.

Turning to see who—or what—had spoken, Liza saw a second shadowy silhouette amongst the trees. It was of a similar height to the first, but rather than some goblin figure, it looked to have regular human proportions and be clothed. Stepping closer, she saw a boy of around her age. She felt as if she ought to know him, but the shadowed face was impossible to place. Nothing in his voice said he recognized her.

"Who are you?" she asked.

"I would guess I am what you came seeking," he replied in the same sweet, innocent voice. "You should not have come here."

"We were curious."

"Were you never taught about the dangers of curiosity? You risk much by your actions, for we are the kindest things that roam the Mount by night…and we are not so kind."

"What do you mean?"

"We offer no direct threat to your kind, merely the occasional necessities of self-preservation. But, there are those who would seek to usurp our position here and would enact any evil to do so."

"Why would they harm me?"

"Need or pleasure. Such beings of darkness are driven by base desires and cruel urges." From the boy's matter-of-fact tone, she had to wonder how far removed from such desires and urges his kind were. As if reading her mind, he added, "We have our own desires and urges that must be fulfilled. Do not imagine we are the sweet-natured fairies you have seen in books." He gave her an endearingly lopsided grin, which almost made her wish she could see him more clearly.

"Will *you* harm me?"

He shrugged. "Maybe. Maybe not."

Liza rather wished he was not quite so honest. She wished she had run away with Mairee.

"Yes. You should have run away with your friend."

She shivered with fear. How did he know her thoughts?

"It is one of our gifts."

"Please, don't!" She burst into tears. Although she couldn't see properly through the tears, she had a horrible suspicion the boy was grinning.

"Calm yourself," he said after a moment's silence.

She fell silent as if entranced.

The boy stepped closer, and a ball of bluish light appeared from nowhere in his left hand, illuminating his face with a ghostly glow. She barely registered the other figure had vanished from the periphery of her vision. She thought she could recognize him, now. He lived over in Crayk; she was certain. She had seen him in church but never spoken to him before nor heard his name.

"Yes, you may have seen me." He responded to her thoughts yet again.

"But, aren't you a... one of the... the Fair Folk?"

He nodded. "You will have heard tell of those who lose their souls."

She felt herself pale, nodded dumbly.

"Sometimes we prefer to take human form rather than our own, and when I say take, I mean *take*."

The terrible fear of realization came over her. Was he keeping her there so such a fate would be hers?

"Yes, you would be useful to us."

"No! No! I won't let you!"

"What makes you think you can stop us, Liza?" He laughed.

She ran, following the rise of the ground to take her back up the hill, praying she would not become totally lost in the woods.

"What makes you think you can escape?"

Running as fast as she could, she dared to look back over her shoulder only once to make sure the *Gollewon Ellee* weren't following her. She could see no sign of any lights at all. The only light was that of the moon from above. The woods were silent save for the crashing of her feet through the undergrowth and the lazy hoots of owls marking her passage. A dark shape flapped across her path, and she thought for a moment she gazed into a pair of large, dark, bottomless eyes, but they were gone in an instant

Ahead of her, she saw lights. Had her pursuers got in front of her? She stumbled to a halt and tripped over a root, falling to her knees. She couldn't help but sob in fear at the thought of the fate about to overtake her. It was too late to run. The lights of the *Gollewon Ellee*, grew close. How had she ever imagined she could outwit or outrun the Fair Folk?

Then, realization struck her. The lights had the orangey flicker of lanterns rather than the unnaturally steady bluish-white glow of the *Gollewon Ellee*. They were not the lights of her pursuers, but of rescuers. The men of the hill had come searching for her. She realized Mairee must have roused the sleeping inhabitants of the Mount in order to summon help.

Liza heard her name called and called back, relief flooding her voice. The friendly lantern lights grew nearer and nearer. She was saved, but Liza knew she would never dare walk through the woods alone again, nor leave her home by night. Never again did she desire to see the *Gollewon Ellee* moving mysteriously through the trees below the wan light of the half-moon.

ONCE UPON A SCREAM

# MR. SHINGLES
*by J. Malcolm Stewart*

"It's down there."

Dante Howell could remember how the whole atmosphere of that late summer's evening had changed around him. That night was the end of his youth. Even twenty years later, he could recall the sweat covering his forehead becoming strangely chilled and the small, quiet wind creeping up his shoulders.

"You sure?" said his younger brother, Nathan, who was better known as Tre.

"Yeah, it should be," said their friend Min-Joon, who in that less-enlightened time was nicknamed Ming. "According to my Grandma's stories, this is the right kind of spot. Flowing water and a deep opening in the earth underneath a bridge."

Dante looked up into the underbelly of the Carquinez Bridge as the night lights began to take effect. The eastbound span of the bridge hummed and rattled with the commuter traffic heading over the waters to Vallejo. Despite the massive latticework of the structure looming over the four of them, it seemed somehow small and far away.

"We doing this or not?" asked Barry, who everyone called Bone. Not just for the stereotypical reasons but also for his knobby elbows which were feared on basketball courts from Hercules to Hayward.

The other three of the group paused and looked at Dante.

It wasn't just that he was the oldest, already thirteen, ahead of Ming and Bone by more than three months and two years older than Tre. It was he had always been the organizer, the ringleader. Good or bad, nothing happened with the four of them until he gave the word.

"Yeah, screw it," Dante said with all the command his voice he could muster. "Let's go."

With that, Bone produced two flashlights from the inside of his hoodie jacket. With a click and smack to one of their sides, the two lights illuminated the moss-covered drainage pipe buried under the Crockett side of the bridge span.

Dante silently thanked God for small favors as the pipe was just high and wide enough for them to enter without crouching.

"Down we go," said Ming.

❦

The damp, musty water soon settled around their ankles, and Dante knew in his heart that the particular pair of Air Force Ones on his feet would never be usable again. The sloshing sound they made was the only thing that disturbed the surrounding darkness as the August night moved steadily away from their backs.

"How far down do we have to go to find him?" he said to Ming.

"I dunno. It depends," Ming replied with a shrug. "According to my grandma, *Dokkaebi* tend to wander during the day and nest at night down in their dens, but remember, that's in Korea."

Tre gave a click of his teeth. "I thought trolls stand on bridges and try to take your head off."

"That's in Europe, dummy," said Dante with contempt. "We aren't dealing with a European type of troll. Right, Ming?"

Ming shrugged again.

"I dunno. My grandma says she's seen the signs that a *Dokkaebi* lives here. Strange footprints, dogs and cats stripped clean down to the bone—but she also says she talks every Sunday night to my great-grandma who died ten years ago."

"Then how do we know this is even gonna work?" said Tre, coming to a halt right in front of Dante. "This is kinda stupid to me."

"Then go home!" said Dante with a kick to his younger brother's shin. "If you're too much of a pussy to be down here, go home now, but I swear, if you tell Mom or Dad anything, I will seriously whip your ass!"

"You guys are gonna scare him away," said Bone in an admonishing whisper.

"Yeah," said Ming. "I thought you were on the same page with this."

"We are," said Dante as he took hold of Tre's right arm. "This is Cee's best chance to live, and we are gonna find this *Dokkaebi,* or this troll, or whatever he is and get him to help her. You said you were gonna help, not act like a fool!"

"I am gonna help!" said Tre with his eyes flashing in the light. "Let go of my arm!"

Dante released Tre with a shove. "Then start walkin' and stop talkin', fool."

"Shhh!" hissed Bone.

The journey continued in silence from that point until the moment Bone discovered the angular crack in the side of the pipe wall. It wasn't much of a gap. It hardly seemed fit for a troll. In fact, another year or two and Dante probably wouldn't even be able to fit through it.

"This should be it," said Ming.

Bone was first to squeeze through as he was the thinnest, followed by Ming and then Tre. Dante had been right in his assessment of his ability to make it in. Even now, jagged edges of pipe and rebar scratched and tore at his jacket. Another loss, just like his shoes.

The worst news was the headroom they had enjoyed had narrowed considerably. No longer able to stand to their full height, Dante, Ming, and Bone were forced to crouch down. Only Tre, being a bit smaller, even for his age, was able to make his way as before.

"It don't smell too good down here," said Bone with a look of disgust.

"Of course it don't," said Dante. "Years and years of everyone dropping their piss and shit down into the Bay until they made them stop? We're probably under ten tons of sewage or worse."

"That's cheerful," Ming said with a snort.

Dante could feel the confidence of the group wavering. He suddenly wasn't feeling all that brave himself.

"C'mon," he said in an attempt to rally up some courage. "This troll's gotta be the one who cracked that pipe and dug this side tunnel. I bet he's not that far away."

"You *think* he's not far," said Tre with a sullen tone.

"Tre, shut up!" Dante hissed.

That brought Dante a few moments of silence. The group made their way down the earthen tunnel slowly, with each step seemingly bringing the walls closer to them.

"I don't think we can go down too much more," said Bone.

Dante let out a rush of air. The roof seemed only an inch or two over his head despite his crouching. Even Tre was bent over almost double. The icy trickle of doubt was beginning to spread over the course of his body.

"What's that?" said Ming in a whisper.

"Huh?" said Tre. "What's what?"

"Shhh!" said Bone.

Dante then heard a slight but steady sound. A sound of ancient metal joints moving with reluctance. The kind of sound a rusty swing set makes in a constant wind.

"It's coming from up ahead," said Ming in such a soft tone Dante was surprised he could be heard. "Maybe fifteen or twenty feet."

The looks of terror on the group's face left little to Dante's imagination.

"Ok," he said, again trying to control the panic in his own voice. "Slowly... Let's not make any quick moves."

The four boys crept forward, each step seemingly more difficult than the last. After taking a turn around a nearly 90-degree bend, a faint light could be seen. The creaking, rusty noise became louder and more distinct. Something was definitely moving around down the pathway from the group.

"Dante..." Tre began.

Dante shot his brother a silent look of accusation. The flaring of his eyes must have communicated the seriousness of his intentions because Tre promptly shut his mouth.

The pause to glare at Tre brought a realization that the ceiling had moved upward enough that Dante could pretty much stand up again. Bone and Ming were already fully upright and pointing to the crouching figure only a few feet away.

Dante could see what looked like a large, naked human. The being was well over six feet, its massive back turned to the group as it huddled before a glowing fire.

It wasn't just the lack of clothes that made Dante pause. The figure's bare back was covered with jagged pieces of bone with glass and wire fragments embedded at different points, jutting out of its skin like some kind of living trash heap.

The figure was swaying lightly, humming some tuneless melody as it busied itself with an unseen task. Each movement of the being brought out the rusty creaking that had enticed them down the pathway. The blending of the humming and the creaking made for a hideous form of hypnosis, rooting each of the group members in their tracks for a long moment.

"Come, come, my friends of light," said the figure's voice, pausing from its tune. "Shall you stare at me all night? Venture forth if hearts shall dare. Round with me the fire share."

The strange statement caused everyone to look at Dante. Somehow, despite the bravado of earlier, actually finding a troll under the Carquinez Bridge had left everyone breathlessly uncertain.

"Okay," he said after a long second. "Thank you."

Dante took a few cautious steps forward. Soon, he found himself sitting down across the fire from the weirdest thing he had ever seen in his then short life.

The creature in front of him was like shattered glass. Even his face was composed of sharp angles and craggy edges as if someone had taken a hammer to a porcelain doll and glued it back willy-nilly. Every portion of his body that Dante could see ended in a point or a peak. Yet within that mess, Dante could see some darkly-set reddish eyes and a narrow slit mouth filled with jagged teeth.

"Brave and brave, now I see," said the creature. "It must be you who that has questions for me."

"Uhhh, yeah... My name's Dante Howell and over there is—are my friends, Ming and Bone, along with my little brother, Tre, and you're right, I do want to talk to you."

"Welcome, welcome!" said the creature with a tremor through his face which resembled a smile. "Welcome now, welcome all!"

Dante gave a wave of his hand for the others to sit down. One by one, with caution, the three boys joined him.

"There, much better is it not?" said the creature. "Join the circle and share the pot! Within is a kingly feast. Boiled seaweed, fish brains... Parts of creatures found on the trash strewn shore. If one taste does not slake thy hunger, I promise there is much, much more."

"Uhh, no thanks," said Dante as his understanding caught up with the creature's method of talking.

"Are you really a *Dokkaebi*?" asked Ming.

"Ahh, a name, a name," said the creature. "The *Dokkaebi* and I are one and the same. A kindred group to one such as I, but far, far across the seas they lie."

"But you're kinda of the same, right?" said Bone as he raised his eyebrows.

"More than more and less than less," said the creature with a creaking shrug. "Many similarities we once possessed. Grants and gifts and holes and fire are the things we under-dwellers do desire."

"Then you can grant wishes?" said Dante, hearing what he had been praying for. "Just like Ming's grandmother's stories?"

"More questions, still?" said the creature with a chuckle. "Of such queries, I soon will have my fill. Not five minutes' peace to eat, I fear, lest all night you bend my ear."

"Oh, I'm sorry," said Dante, realizing the group's rudeness. "We'll let you eat, Mr...? Uhh, Mr...?"

"Ahh, yes," said the creature as he pulled a steaming mass of gunk out of the pot with his sharpened fingers. "A name to serve and name to claim. To be known by and be known again. Please take note with utmost care, Mr. Shingles is the name I bear."

"Mr. Shingles?" said Tre with a half-squeak.

"Aye, 'tis my name, all right."

The creature proceeded to slurp down the concoction between his fingers. "Are you certain you wish not a bite?"

"No, thank you again," said Dante as he tried to conceal his disgust.

"Fair, fair, more for me," said Mr. Shingles with a sigh. "A being alone perhaps I shall always be. To your business then. Far down the hole you've come, I suppose for a boon. Perhaps it's for best that you tell me soon. What troubles such a young man's heart so fresh and fair? Why have you come hence into my lair?"

"It's our sister, Cee!" said Tre suddenly. "She's dying, and you have to help her!"

"Shut up, Tre!" said Dante as he followed his words with a punch to his brother's arm.

"Ow!" cried Tre. "Stop being a dickhead, Dante. I'm just trying to tell him why we're here."

"Ahh, I see," said Mr. Shingles as he gathered more goo between his fingers. "A tragedy writ large and wide, a family soon separated by death's divide. A shining life too soon snuffed out, unless saved by the love of a brother, so devout."

"Uhh, yes, sir," said Dante. "I mean, my brother's right in the sense that my sister, Cecilia... Well, she's really sick. They, the doctors, I mean, they say there's nothing they can do for her anymore."

"Yes, this sad tale is true," said Mr. Shingles with a shake of his head. "Soon, her eyes will fade and no longer will her chest arise. You will witness as all the light within her dies."

The creature slurped down more of the hideous stew and licked his fingers. "A shame and a shame. I too know the burn of burden's flame. To lose love and have none to bear your name. Upon you alone is shouldered eternity's claim."

"But you can help us, right?" said Tre. "I mean, you trolls grant wishes and favors and stuff like that, don't you?"

"Yes, yes," said Mr. Shingles. "Yes and yes, we in ages past gave favor and rest to those who did worthy deeds. Who solved great riddles or who met our needs, but always for a boon or gift, there was an exchange of dual benefit. Something you need given in return for a goal of mine. This leads to a dealing both fair and sublime."

"Do you need money?" said Dante with trepidation.

"Tosh!" said the creature as he raised a hand to his chest. "Such as I have no need of such trivial fare. An equal exchange is my only care."

"That's perfect!" said Tre. "We only got sixteen dollars between us, anyway."

Dante gave his brother a death glare.

Mr. Shingles gave another shattered smile.

"My own needs I will not speak of again. However, since thy current need is so dire, much must be done to gain what you desire."

"What?" said Dante. "What do we have to do? We'll do anything we can possibly do to save Cee."

"Good, good," said the creature. "A good heart I see within you, Dante. A heart loving and loyal in midst of the fray. Also with you, friends good and wise. With you four the answer lies."

"What do we need to do?" said Ming with an air of caution.

"Follow the pattern of what I say," said Mr. Shingles as he raised a finger. "Do it all with no delay. Tell no one of this deed and take careful heed. These are the items that you shall need."

The creature leaned in closer toward Dante.

"A bit of hair from thy sister's head, some steaming piss from an infant's bed, the small, right finger from a screaming man. Bring these all and do this work, I can."

"Uhh, ok..." said Dante, once again letting the creature's words seep into his mind. "How are we gonna get all that?"

"Delay not!" said Mr. Shingles more firmly than before. "These things must be done with haste to the tittle. Despite the difficulty of my riddle, not one element must be left to lie. Hair, blood, and piss must be taken away from sight of prying eyes. Now go! Four more suns and thy sister dies."

Dante and the three others scrambled back up the passageway. Not a word was exchanged until the four boys stood back outside in the cooling night air underneath the Carquinez Bridge.

"I don't know about this," said Ming. "Did you hear him? How are we going to do everything he wants us to do?"

"There's a way to do everything, Ming," said Dante. "Trust me, I will find a way to figure it out."

"Was that even freaking real?" said Bone.

"It has to be," said Dante as he leaned back against the dusty hillside. "It has to be."

༄ঙ

It was nearly eleven o'clock when Dante and Tre took off their shoes and made their way through the kitchen door. The hope was Mom and Dad would be catching a rare moment of rest by that time. Like a lot of other kinds of hope in those days, it died quickly.

"Dante and Tre!" said his mother's voice before he could even close the door. "Where the hell have you two been?"

"Awh, man," said Tre with despair.

A quick whack from Mom came to the back of Dante's head, followed by an equal sharp strike to his brother. She was now directly in front of them while Dad stood in the frame of the kitchen's inner entryway, Pastor Burns at his side.

"Answer your mother!" said Dad with a barely held fury. "What do you two think you're doing sneaking out till this time of night? We've got enough worries! And dammit all, Dante! What the hell did you do to your jacket?"

Dante felt the hot sting of shame pool and spread over his face. He really thought they wouldn't be noticed sneaking out tonight to find the troll, not with Cee coming home just that morning.

The mix of anger and suffering on his parents' faces troubled Dante deeply. In that instant, he almost let the true story of their strange quest leave his lips.

"We're sorry, Mom," said Tre again without warning. "We just went for some two-on-two with Ming and Bone. We thought after dinner..."

Dante felt himself recover enough to back Tre's story.

"We didn't think you'd notice. I mean, you need to get some rest. We were gonna sit up with Cee after we got back."

The look on Mom's face proved she was not swayed.

"You're not to leave this house without permission again! Understand me?"

"Yes, ma'am," the brothers both said quickly.

"Nathan, Cheri," said Pastor Burns as he moved toward the boys, "why don't you go back in the living room and let me talk to the boys outside?"

In a single motion, Pastor Burns took the boys outside to the porch. The three of them stood in the harsh yellow of the porch light for a good long moment before Pastor Burns let loose a sigh.

"This hasn't been easy for you two," he said in a low, even tone. "I know you're suffering just like your mom and dad, and you need some relief, too. I see that. This hurts everyone. Everyone loves your sister."

Pastor Burns' words couldn't have been truer. Everyone did love Cee. Co-valedictorian of her high school, head of the BSU, Cheer squad leader, heading into her sophomore year at Berkeley. Then the news came, Hodgkin's lymphoma, Stage IV spread all across her body like some wind-driven wildfire. Tests, treatments, drugs, all ineffective and at the end of it all, sent home by the doctors to die like some unwanted pet.

"Your parents need your strength and your support," said Pastor Burns. "You need to be close to home. You have to lend them your strength right now, boys. I know it's hard, but sometimes, we need to do the hard things to make it through."

"Yes, sir," Dante managed to mumble.

"Try to forgive your mom?" said Pastor Burns with a small smile. "Try to forgive everyone for not knowing how to do the things they should right now. Let's go back in."

It wasn't that Pastor Burns didn't mean well. Everyone meant well with their thoughts, and words, and prayers. The problem was someone needed to *do* something.

Inside was the same as it had been for months, Mom crying, Dad yelling, Pastor Burns praying, and Cee dying by degrees in front of their very eyes.

Dante and Tre sat with her in the downstairs bedroom while the adults did what they normally did. He focused in on the wispy, fading form of his sister, her eyes gaunt and shaded, her discolored skin bumpy and dry.

It was so unlike the vibrant, laughing older giant who used to pick him up and carry him around the house on her hip. This shell on the bed was nearly dead. Like Mr. Shingles had said, it would be soon, maybe just a few days.

"Do you think it will work?" said Tre in a half-whisper.

Dante took a deep breath.

"Like I said, it has to."

"Can we trust Mr. Shingles?" said Tre with a frown.

"I think so," said Dante. "The stories we read say that trolls keep their word. Besides, he doesn't seem so bad. He's like a fucked up version of Santa Claus and Dr. Seuss."

That brought a quick smile to Tre's face, but it faded when he turned back to Cee.

It was at that moment Dante's fate was firmly cast. He was going to be the one to save Cee. Goddammit, unlike everyone else, he was going to do *something*.

❧⬥❧

The next few days passed far too quickly. It proved more difficult than Dante had expected to gather up some of Cee's hair. What little remained on her head was hard to find and gather off of her pillow. It also could only be done when Mom or Dad wasn't in the room, which was increasingly rare. That took almost a full day.

The next item on the list also proved difficult. Bone had to baby sit his nephew for nearly another full day before he could successfully capture the toddler's urine. Then, the jelly jar full of piss had to be sealed and carefully hidden in the bushes between Bone and Dante's houses.

Then, after some planning and arguments and more planning, came the finger.

❧⬥❧

It was more than three days later that Dante and the others were found crouching in the high-hill chaparral near the Pomona exit on Hwy 80. Tre sat at the highest point, using the night vision binoculars Bone's Dad got from the Gulf War to scan the eastbound traffic. Bone, to the back and left, crouched ready with another item from his father's tools, a baseball bat. Last, in the pocket of Dante's white 49ers starter jacket, was a pair of wire cutters.

Ming was next to Dante, ready to assume the needed position in the crucial moments before the springing of their trap.

The scent of that night, salty and sour, made the chilled air of that 3:00 a.m. hour taste like onrushing death. Dante could recall the churning of his stomach as fear, anxiety, and anger all fought for room in the same, tiny space.

Time was growing short. They could afford no more mistakes.

"I see someone" called Tre from his upper position.

"Are you sure?" said Dante, letting his annoyance show in his voice.

Last night's set trap had been ruined by Tre mistaking a bigger, graying woman for a useful candidate. Dante had saved the day by playing off the whole thing as a misadventure of dumb kids messing around on the freeway.

It still had resulted in the two of them having to take a trip to Contra Costa Regional Hospital in lieu of her calling the cops. Lucky for them she was a grandma. Equally as fortunate, they had been able to sneak out on her when she went to the admit desk with their paperwork.

"Yes, I'm sure this time!" said Tre. "Young white dude in a Beamer, all by himself. About two miles away."

Perfect, thought Dante, male, young and probably able to afford some hospital bills. He sprang to his feet with tap to Ming's shoulder.

"Go! Go!"

With that said, Ming ran to assume his position in the middle lane of the highway.

Dante prayed that Tre had remembered Bone's tutoring from the other day on how to read the range finder. If he had gotten the wrong measurement and the oncoming car was too close— Well, then there would be three funerals.

Armed with his flashlight, Dante began his frantic arm-waving. The headlights of the BMW were coming down the center lane.

"Stop! Stop!"

The onrushing lights stayed steady in their approach toward Dante. For a moment, he saw his parents' mourning faces at his graveside, gaunt and leeched of color. Then, he heard the sound of screeching tires and the sweeping explosion of dust and debris on asphalt.

With only feet to spare, the BMW came to a stop, its powerful engine roaring down to a muted purr.

A shadowy figure appeared outside the driver's door behind the glare of the headlights.

"Holy shit! Do you know how close you came to me killing you? For fuck's sake, what do you think you're doing in the middle of the God-damned freeway?"

"Help! My friend is sick and needs help! I dared him to run across the lanes, but he just fell down!"

Dante turned his light on the balled-up form of Ming, who added in some helpful moaning down on the ground.

Dante could see the man stiffen at the sight of Ming. Shock and surprise had caused him to stop, but now the cold trickle of fear was seeping into his face.

"You stay put. I'm gonna get my phone and call for an ambulance."

Dante could hear the suspicion rising in his voice and likely there would have been no phone call to anybody until he was miles away from the scene.

It was too late for escape, however. Bone's signal to strike had come with the turning of Dante's light onto Ming. With a speed of a jungle cat, he had come from his hiding place, around the back side of the car and behind the driver.

Just as their target was ducking down back into the driver's side, Bone delivered a blow right to the center of the man's shoulder blades. Dante heard a short cry of pain and horror leave the man's mouth almost in sync with the fleshly thud of the bat strike. With that done, the driver hit the pavement face first with one leg still in the driver's door.

Bone in the next instant was on top of their victim, using his feared elbows to drive the man's chin into the pavement. Dante and Ming moved as one, with Ming twisting the man's arm behind his back while Dante jammed the open wire cutters around the outside of his right little finger.

He paused for a heartbeat to gather his breath and strength. Then with the force of his two hands on the wire cutter's handle, he brought the blades together.

The resistance pressure he felt was overcome in a second. A slight crunch and tug was followed by a sharp scream and a flow of blood from their victim.

Bone gave a quick jab of his elbow into the face of the now squirming man.

"Car! Car!" cried Tre from his lookout perch.

With a haste borne of final desperation, Dante scooped up the newly freed finger and stuffed it into the waiting sandwich baggie.

Without another word, the four boys ran from the freeway and the hillside down the Pomona exit and into darkness.

❦

It was a good hour before the recovery of the jelly jar from the bush and Cee's hair from the backyard was complete. It was another thirty minutes more of walking and climbing down to the entry to Mr. Shingle's lair. Despite the hundreds of feet of rock and dirt that separated Dante from the surface, he could almost feel the rising sun coming up around him and the others.

Down the hole they went, past the ragged gash, down the tunnel, and around the bend. At the end, they found Mr. Shingles waiting, again humming a gleeful, toneless tune as he stirred his pot, a wicked grin sliced into his face.

Dante presented him the three items they had collected without fanfare. Mr. Shingles took them and added them to the boiling pot without halting his humming. His stirring became more animated until Dante saw he was whisking together in the pot a great pasty concoction of yellow slime.

A sharp, rank odor filled the cavern. Mr. Shingles put a portion of the goo into the jelly jar where the urine had been stored.

"Take! Take!" said the creature with a nod. "Take this to your sister before it is too late. Three drops will change her fate. The rest apply over the next days that lie ahead. Do this with care... If not, she shall be dead."

"Yes, sir," said Dante taking a hold of the strange potion. "I'll make sure."

The rest of the group had started back up the tunnel way when Mr. Shingles stopped Dante with a light touch on his shoulder.

"Thanks be to you, Dante. You have done a dark deed with resolve. A task which only few hardy souls are called. Now, you have both our torments at last resolved."

The creature leaned in toward Dante's face.

"But my son, in years and years hence, when you find yourself burning in the cold daylight of memory's glare... Recall always that our exchange of deeds was in all ways of honor, promise, and equity, in truth, completely fair."

"Okayyy," said Dante with an uncertain nod.

The words of Mr. Shingles stayed in the back of Dante's mind as he made his way back to the surface.

❧❧

The group dispersed without words at the top of the hill. Bone threw up on Ming's shoes as they left. Dante had no time to worry about their mind-state, however. The sky was beginning to whiten with the dawn.

He and Tre made their way home and scaled up the shed to their window. After checking to make sure Mom was in bed, they crept past their sleeping father in the living room and to Cee's bedside. Dante had Tre grab a spoon and as carefully as he could, he measured out a portion of the potion.

With a shaking hand, he put three drops on Cee's lips, one at a time, rubbing her cracked lips with the liquid.

"Is it working?" said Tre in an urgent half-whisper. "Is it working?"

"I don't know yet," said Dante. "I don't know."

"What are we gonna do if it doesn't work?" said Tre, saying the unsayable. "What if Mr. Shingles lied to us?"

"No," said Dante with a strange feeling of peace. "No, he wouldn't do that. He's gonna keep his word. We just have to wait."

So they did just that, waited through the pale, early September sunrise while Mr. Shingles' words repeated over and over in Dante's mind.

ॐ

The next few days saw a miracle. The day after the first drops, Cee somehow strengthened. After a few more days and a few more drops, she actually regained consciousness and awareness for the first time in weeks. By the end of the next week, she was sitting up in bed, talking with family and well-wishers like a child recovered from a bout with the flu.

Somehow, Cee was back, happy, healthy, and perfect. It hadn't even taken all of the concoction that Mr. Shingles had given him.

Mom cried tears of joy all that week. Dad cried too, but tried not to show it. Pastor Burns and the whole church crowded into the house, seemingly at the same time, laughing, singing, and praising Jesus the whole way. Everyone seemed sure that some great mysterious, grand miracle had been worked by their persistent prayer and vigil. Pastor Burns was positive of that fact.

Whenever the praising got to a certain frenzy, Dante couldn't help but give Tre a knowing smile and think of the now half-empty jelly jar buried behind piles of comics and video games in their closet.

Even through the haze of the years spent lying, and hiding, and regretting, Dante couldn't help but recall the pride he had felt. He had saved Cee. It had been because of him she had been saved.

It was on the Saturday of the following week that things fell apart.

Mom and Dad finally felt okay enough to leave Cee's bedside and do some normal stuff like housework and grocery shopping. Dante had finally been able to get some quiet time with Cee to play their all-time favorite time killer, checkers. Tre was somewhere in the back talking on the phone.

"Your move, Big Dee," said Cee, flashing her renewed signature smile.

Dante was preparing to be kinged for the third time when Tre rushed in and grabbed him by the arm.

"I gotta tell you something."

"Hey! What the hell? I'm just—"

Tre pulled at Dante's arm even harder.

"I gotta tell you something."

Dante allowed himself to be moved into the hall while his sister gave the two of them a slight frown.

"What?" he finally said to Tre after the pair settled near the closet in the laundry room.

"It's bad, Dante," his brother said in a nervous whisper. "The cops came by Ming's house."

Tre's words gave Dante a hard pause.

"The cops? Why would they come to Ming's house?"

"He said they checked the incident record at the hospital, and they saw the night you guys got taken there. He wrote down his real name and address on the paperwork! Ever since the guy whose finger got cut off made the news, the cops have been checking around. Ming doesn't know what to do."

"What do you mean? He can't tell them anything. We'll all get caught."

"His parents are freaking out. They want him to tell the cops everything he did."

"Shit! He *can't* talk to them."

"Hey, hurry it up!" said Cee, calling from down the hall. "I'm not done whipping your booty up in here!"

"What are we going to do, Dante?"

Dante left that question unanswered and returned to Cee's bedside. As his heart pounded in his chest, he watched as Cee used her kinged checkers to jump his perfectly positioned pair of kings.

"A lesson given is a lesson learned," said Cee with a smile of triumph. "Mess with Cee and you will get burned."

At Cee's word's, Dante felt his pounding heart sink.

"Hah!" she said. "That rhymes!"

The strange last words of Mr. Shingles again returned to Dante's mind. That moment of sheer panic was like nothing he had felt before or since.

"Do me a favor, Dee, and scratch my lower back," said his sister leaning forward. "For some reason, it's itching like crazy."

Even after the passing of the many years, Dante Howell still could recall how much effort it took for him not to scream when he saw the shafts of sharp bone sticking through the back of his sister's nightgown.

# THE BOY AND HIS TEETH
*by V. E. Battaglia*

There once was a young boy who lived with his mother in a small town called Dreeg. His mother had been a receptionist for a time until the business in which she had worked closed down. They soon fell on hard times, the young boy and his mother, as it had become very difficult for her to find a new job. They became poorer and poorer until their nice clothes had become rags and they could no longer afford their pleasant little apartment.

Fortunately, her kindly parents said, "There is no need to fret. We have plenty of room for two and more than enough for four. You can come live with us."

And so the poor boy and his mother moved in with his grandparents. They lived in a single room together, mother and son, he on the bed and she on the floor, for she said her son would never be made to sleep like an animal. They went on this way for some time and the boy, though comfortable in a bed, could never fall asleep. In his dreams, he heard the taunts of the children at school.

> *Poor little rag boy*
> *Sleeping with his mommy*
> *Daddy never loved him*
> *So he left him for dead*

Even worse was lying awake at night and listening to the agony of his mother's crying. One night, he heard her talking to herself through her tears.

"My poor son, my poor family. If only I had some money, if only, if only."

The boy said to himself, "Don't worry, Mom. I will find a way to make some money." He gritted his teeth so tightly, one of them came loose.

The next day, he played with the loosened tooth with his tongue. Scared, he ran to his grandfather and said, "Grandpa, Grandpa, I think I'm hurt!"

The kindly old man grew concerned and said to him, "Why, grandson, whatever happened?"

"My tooth! It's falling out!" The boy opened his mouth and revealed his loosened tooth.

His grandfather called him closer and delicately placed a finger upon the tooth, "Well," he said and gave it a wiggle. "You're not hurt at all, my boy. You're losing a tooth."

"This is awful!" The young boy said, shocked, "If I lose my teeth, how will I eat?"

The old man laughed. "Awful? No, no. This is a great moment. Your first tooth is falling out. Now newer, stronger teeth will grow in, and you know about the tooth fairy, right?"

"No, Grandpa. Who's that?"

"Well," he said and placed the boy on his lap. "The Tooth Fairy is a magical being who collects the teeth of children from beneath their pillows in their sleep and rewards them with money."

"Really? With lots of money? I don't know."

"You'll just have to place that tooth under your pillow before you sleep and find out."

And so the boy went to school, and the children picked on him for his clothes and his hair, and when he got home he ran upstairs and played with the tooth in the mirror, wiggling it to and fro, harder and harder until it was so loose he simply plucked it from his mouth.

He ran to his grandfather and showed him the tooth, and then he ran up to his bedroom and placed it beneath his pillow. Then he told his mom as she tucked him in to sleep.

"Don't worry. We'll have money soon, Mom, and then we can go and get our own apartment and buy nice clothes and be happy again."

She kissed her son and said, "One day, my son. One day. I'll see to it, but don't you worry about that. That's the job of an adult. We just have to be patient, and we'll get what we deserve."

The boy could barely close his eyes from excitement but he remembered his grandfather's words. He knew that the tooth fairy would only come as he slept. So, he shut his eyes tight and fell asleep to the sound of his mother's crying once again.

In the morning, the young boy woke with a start and grabbed underneath his pillow. In place of the tooth, he found a five dollar bill. He looked at the money in shock and ran down to his mother.

"Mom, Mom, the tooth fairy came and brought me money! We can use it to get our own apartment and buy nice clothes and be happy."

His mother gave a weak smile and said, "Thank you for being so sweet, but I can't take your money. It's *my* job to take care of *you*. Besides, we would need *much* more than that. One day, we will have the money. One day."

The boy ran to his grandfather and said, "Grandpa! The tooth fairy left me money, but it's not enough! How do I get her to leave more?"

"You have to be patient and wait like a good boy. You will lose more teeth, and the tooth fairy will reward you once more. That's the only way."

The boy checked his teeth and found that none of them were loose. Then a thought came to him and he asked, "What about adult teeth, Grandfather? Will the tooth fairy take those?"

"No, they must be the teeth of a young person."

So the boy went to school, and the children made fun of him for his clothes, and his hair, and every day he went home and tugged at his teeth with his hands, but they never came loose.

He soon decided he needed a tool to help it along, so he grabbed a hammer and pliers from the garage and hammered the pliers around one of his teeth and ripped it out of his own mouth. The boy screamed out in pain, and his mother, hearing his cries, rushed to his aid.

Upon seeing her son bloodied and hurt, she fell to her knees in tears, wrapped her arms around him and said, "My god, what's happened to you?"

Through tears, the boy said, "I tore out one of my teeth. We need the money."

His mother sobbed and said to him, "Son, this is not the way. You can't hurt yourself. Please, promise me no more of this."

The young boy, feeling bad, promised her it would not happen again. Then he cleaned himself up and brought the tooth upstairs. *Now we will have the money we need*, he thought to himself, and he placed the tooth beneath his pillow. That night, he had trouble sleeping from the pain but, knowing he had to, he forced his eyes closed and fell asleep to the sound of his mother's crying once again.

In the morning, the young boy woke with a start from the pain in his mouth and grabbed underneath his pillow. In place of the tooth, he found another five dollar bill. He took the money and ran down to his mother.

"Mom, Mom, the tooth fairy came and brought me more money! We can use it to get our own apartment, and buy nice clothes, and be happy."

His mother gave a weak smile and shook her head. "Son, thank you, but I already told you, I can't take your money. Besides, we would need *much* more than that. One day, we will have the money. One day. You have to be patient."

Disappointed, the boy ran to his grandfather and said, "Grandpa, the tooth fairy left me money again but it's still not enough. Can I catch the tooth fairy and explain that I need more money?"

His grandfather said, "No, that is why she only comes in your sleep."

"Has anyone ever tried?"

"Of course. Many times. The tooth fairy cannot be caught."

The boy went upstairs and checked his teeth and found none of them loose, and he knew he could no longer pull them out on his own.

So, the boy went to school, and the children continued to make fun of him for his clothes and his hair, and every day he went home and tugged at his teeth, but they were never loose.

One day, the boy went to school and waited for the biggest bully in his class to begin making fun of him, and the boy made fun of him right back until the two ended up in a fight after school. The bully pushed and shoved and hit the boy many times until his nose was bleeding and one of his teeth was knocked loose.

The poor boy, knowing his plan had worked, went home, and when his mother saw him she began to cry.

"What happened today at school?" she asked him.

"The kids at school are mean to me. They make fun of me. So, I made fun back, and I got into a fight."

"I'm sorry they are mean to you, son, but being mean back is not the answer. I don't want you to get hurt. Please, promise me, no more of this."

The young boy, feeling quite bad, promised her it would not happen again. Then he went upstairs and yanked the loosened tooth from his sore gums. *Now we will definitely have the money we need*, he thought, and he placed the tooth beneath his pillow. That night, he had trouble sleeping from the pain, but knowing he had to, forced his eyes closed and fell asleep to the sound of his mother's crying once again.

In the morning, the young boy woke with a start and grabbed underneath his pillow. In place of the tooth, he found yet another five dollar bill. He took the money and ran down to his mother.

"Mom, Mom, the tooth fairy came and brought me even more money! We can use it to get our own apartment and buy nice clothes, and we can finally be happy."

His mother let out a heavy sigh and said, "Thank you for being so sweet, but I've already told you I will not take your money. One day, we will have the money. One day. Be patient. No more of this nonsense."

Frustrated, the boy ran to his grandfather and said, "Grandfather, the tooth fairy left me money again, but it is still not enough." The boy sat a while and finally asked, "What If I put another person's tooth beneath my pillow? Will I get rewarded for that?"

His grandfather gave him a grave look and said, "Boy. Never, ever place another's tooth beneath your pillow. You cannot take that which is not yours. That is a very evil thing to do."

The boy tried to ask why, but his grandfather would hear no more of the subject. So he went upstairs and checked his teeth and found none of them loose, and he knew he could no longer get into fights to lose his teeth.

The boy went to school, and the children made fun of him for his clothes and his hair, and every day he went home and tugged at his teeth, but they were never loose.

After many weeks, the boy became angrier and angrier. He could not understand why he should have to wait so long to make enough money to help his mother. He and his mother had been patient, he thought. Why shouldn't they be allowed to be happy? And why should those other kids, those mean kids who had made fun of him so often, be allowed to make money from their teeth? It just wasn't fair, and that made him even angrier.

One day, the boy waited outside of school after classes let out, and he followed one of the smaller bullies that made fun of him as he walked home from school. When they were alone, the boy tackled him and pulled out the pliers and hammer from his bag.

"I need a tooth, and I'm not sorry to take it from you." He pulled a tooth from the screaming boy's mouth and ran home.

That night, he laid the tooth in his fist and placed his hand under his pillow. This time, when the tooth fairy came, she would have to wake him up.

In spite of the excitement of the day, the boy had no trouble falling asleep.

The boy woke in the middle of the night with his empty hand on his pillow. He knew he must have moved it in his sleep and immediately checked under his pillow for the tooth. This time, in place of money, he found a hole in his bed. The boy checked on his mother and, finding her asleep, lifted his pillow. The hole in his bed was growing slowly, getting bigger and bigger, and it glowed from somewhere deep within. The boy gathered his nerve and hovered over the hole. He stared down a seemingly endless burrow with rocky walls and a foggy glow at its bottom, and he could hear a faint sound from somewhere deep within, a sound like crying or maybe laughing.

The boy leaned down close to the hole and called softly, "Hello?" He received no response. He leaned closer and called out again, louder. "Hello?" Still, he heard nothing but distant noise. The boy stuck his head in the hole and yelled, "Hello?"

The hole echoed back at him with an angry growl, and a hand shot up, grabbed him by the face, and dragged him inside, dragging him down, down, down to the bottom of the glowing hole until he landed in a strange chair at its bottom. It felt bumpy and sharp beneath him. When he looked, he saw it was made of teeth.

Now in a panic, the boy looked around the fog covered room and, in the distance, saw a figure approaching. It floated toward him wistfully until its grotesque, toothless face sat directly opposite his.

"Thank you," the tooth fairy said and gave him a skeletal grin which seemed to be changing right before his eyes.

"Thanks for what?" the boy asked through tears.

"For freeing me."

With that, the tooth fairy reached a desiccated hand out to him. Against his will, his mouth opened wide, and the tooth fairy started plucking his teeth out one by one. With each tooth he lost, the tooth fairy grew one to match in its own mouth. The boy watched helplessly as the tooth fairy's skin began to change and grow healthful and colorful while his own skin shriveled and grew dead. Then the tooth fairy's hair grew back in, a brilliant blonde, long and flowing, and the boy's hair turned gray and thin, popped out from his head, and fell around him in patches. By the end, the boy found himself staring at a beautiful young girl.

"What happened to me?" the boy asked, his voice filled with gravel.

"Your greed and anger have brought you here as my own once did. You sought to steal from others that which was rightfully theirs. Now, you will be a servant, giving away what you wanted most every day. You will start with pennies, as I did, and after 100 years you will leave nickels, then dimes and so on. You will do this until someone takes your place."

Then the girl disappeared in a flourish of light, leaving the tooth fairy who was once a poor boy alone to serve his sentence and await the next unfortunate child whose greed and impatience convinced them to take something that wasn't theirs.

# THE OTHER DAUGHTER
*by Adam L. Bealby*

"Can I help you?"

She looked to be about twelve, fringe bangs and long blonde hair framing an open face. Cute-as-a-button upturned nose. Was she wearing a Brownie uniform? No, too old to be a Brownie. Some sort of plain Hessian dress. More sackcloth, really. These days it was impossible to keep up with modern fashions.

"Hello? I said, can I help you, luv?"

The girl stood on the doorstep with a thin sad smile fixed to her lips.

"Hello, Mum," she said at last.

"Oh dear…"

"Guess this must be a shock," she said.

"You could say that." It was her daughter, Hannah. Ami hadn't recognized her. How bad was that? But it had been so long since Hannah had worn her hair in that way, and look, she still had freckles. Ami could never be sure whether she'd outgrown them because she always had that heavy goth makeup on, and she'd put her age down wrong. Hannah was fourteen, but this Hannah looked younger, fresher. The way she'd looked before. The *old* Hannah. God, how she missed her.

"Can I come in?"

But…that couldn't be right. Hannah, the *new* Hannah was upstairs, wasn't she? Ami could hear the dull animal-throb of her music through the ceiling. Unless she'd given herself a make-over and snuck out the back door and round to the front? A cruel joke, maybe? If it was, Hannah was talking to her at least, which was more than could be said of the last few months.

Ami gestured into the kitchen. "Of course, luv. It's your house as well, isn't it?"

Inside, Hannah looked about with wonderment in her eyes, like she'd never seen a kitchen before. She had a strappy bag with her, Hessian, like the dress. She put the bag on the kitchen table. It clanked. She sat down.

Ami wiped her hands on her apron. She'd been rolling bread dough before the doorbell rang. She busied herself with the kettle.

"Is your boyfriend still here?" She glanced at the thrumming ceiling. "I presume this…*change* is meant to surprise me? Shock me, you said. Don't get me wrong, I like the new look. I do, but luv, what's this really all about?"

"It's not me that's changed," Hannah said. "It's *you*. I suppose you've had to, dealing with that little monster up there. I know what they're like. Trouble from start to finish."

"I'm not sure I understand," Ami said.

Hannah made a sound of disbelief at the back of her throat. "You mean you still don't get it? Golly, Mum, how do I break this to you? The girl upstairs? She's *still* upstairs, but she isn't your real daughter. I am. *I'm* Hannah."

Ami's hands shook as she poured the hot water. *Drugs.* Had to be. These days all the kids were on them. She finished up and carried the steaming mugs over to the table.

"Is that how it's going to be, then?" she said, sitting opposite. "More silly games?"

"Did you really not have a clue? I mean, I'm your *daughter*. The fruit of your loins. You're supposed to know me better than you know yourself. All these months, did you never think? Did you never wonder why she looked so different, why she acted so different? And the smell! Oh gosh, Mum! Did you never wonder about the *smell?*"

Ami looked long and hard at her daughter. *The old Hannah.* How had she changed so quickly? It felt like only fifteen minutes ago she'd come shambling into the house with that Neanderthal boyfriend of hers—Gerp or Goik or whatever he was calling himself these days. They'd grabbed a couple of cans of coke from the fridge and gone shambling upstairs, and how come she had her old hair back? Was she wearing extensions?

Over the muffled *thump-crump* of the music Ami heard a girl laughing upstairs.

"Hannah?" she said, drinking in the girl sitting in her kitchen, seeing her properly for the very first time.

"Did you ever love me?" Hannah asked. There were tears in her eyes.

"Of course! Honestly, I never stopped!" Ami reached across the table and cupped Hannah's hand. "It really is you, isn't it?"

"So why did you never come get me? I *waited* for you. All that time, thinking Mum was coming to the rescue, because it sure wasn't going to be Dad, was it? But you never came!"

Ami welled up. "Hannah, luv, believe me, I didn't know! I don't know why I didn't know, and I can't begin to tell you how bad I feel about that.

If it helps, it all makes sense now. There was so much that didn't add up. My Hannah, she would never act like that. *Never*. I thought it was me. I thought you were growing up, and I was having just the worst imaginable time letting go, especially with your dad not being around. I thought I was losing my mind!"

Hannah seemed to accept this. "Well, I'm back now."

"Yes. Yes, you are, luv, and I'm going to make it up to you. You wait and see."

"But what are we going to do about…"

"*Her?*" Ami motioned at the thrumming ceiling.

"Don't think of it as a 'her'," Hannah said. "That's a changeling, Mum."

"A changeling?"

"You know, a child substitute."

"Fairies?"

"Trolls, actually."

"Oh, dear."

Hannah took a deep breath. "Usually they swap the kid out when it's a baby, but it wasn't that way with me. They did the swap when I was walking back from school one day. You know that bit of parkland with the clump of trees off London Road? Yeah, there. Trolls are basically lazy creatures. They're not entirely evil. Cruel yes, but mostly just lazy. They can't be bothered with poopy nappies and sleepless nights and then the endless years of back-chat, so usually they get some humans to rear their kid for them. Sort of like fostering."

"What happens to the human child?" Ami asked.

"Usually the trolls eat them, but like I said, it wasn't that way with me. It was far worse than that. The ones who took me, they'd tried their hand at raising a kid, and it had proved too much for them. So they sent this troll kid back to you all nicely packaged up in a glamour, and that left them with this little human girl, all sinew and bone. Hardly an appetizer, really. So they set me to work. I had to sweep out the den and boil the nettle tea, mend their clothes, pick lice out of their hair, and chop logs to keep the fire going through the winter.

"Mostly the trolls slept. Sometimes they'd hunt. Raw meat, you see. It's the only thing that'll get them out of bed in the morning. They love the stuff. Even then they'd rather take the easy route. When they could, the trolls would steal chickens from the local farm, or they'd come shambling back with some maggot-infested road-kill. No matter how hard I tried to keep it clean, the den always stank. Least I got good with a needle and thread. I made this dress. The bag, too."

Hannah, the *other* Hannah, couldn't even work out how to put her dirty clothes in the laundry basket.

"The trolls tormented me," Hannah continued. "They'd tell me how you'd given me away because I was such a horrible kid. They told me how close we were to your house, just a few miles. It might as well have been a million. The den was dug into the ground around the roots of this old oak tree. There was only one way in and out, and they kept this boulder in the way, and I wasn't strong enough to move it. They said I would die in their service, grow blind and toothless, picking lice out of their hair until the very end."

Hannah sipped her tea. "I bided my time. See, it was always going to happen. One night those lazy trolls were too lazy to roll the boulder back in place. Their laziness got me there, and their laziness got me out. At the very end, it was them who were blind and toothless, not me."

Her free hand crept into the bag on the table and came out brandishing a pair of eight-inch scissors.

Ami reared up. "What are those for?"

"You said it yourself. 'What are we going to do about her?' No. No, it was me who'd said that. Wasn't it? Well this is what we're going to do, Mum. *To* her. To her boyfriend. They're both as bad as each other. Iron, Mum. Trolls hate the stuff. 'Specially when it's sticking out of their black hearts. You'd think they'd have given me a pair of plastic scissors to do the sewing or something, but no! Like I said, *lazy*."

A dread like hoarfrost stole up upon Ami. She wouldn't lose a child again, even if it was the bad one.

"No," she said. "There must be another way."

Hannah's expression was so pitiless it scared her. "You have to be strong, Mum. Now more than ever."

Ami tried to think of the future, of the time she would spend with her new daughter, same as the old one. Getting to know her all over again. Nights in with toasted marshmallow swirl ice-cream, girly chats, and schlocky rom-coms. Matching slippers and make-up tips, spa treatments, and shopping trips. Just being able to talk again. To someone. *Anyone.*

"Quickly then, before I change my mind."

She led the way up the stairs, but each step she climbed, it was like the altitude was ratcheting up. She was riding Charlie's Glass Elevator, and the oxygen, at these rare heights was as thin as her ex-husband's excuses. She remembered the arguments. God, how she remembered the arguments. Hannah had left them to it, scampering off like a timid little field mouse. When it was finally over, in the aftermath of the divorce, she'd come crawling out from under the wreckage, and Ami had thought then, *she's changed.* She blamed David. Hannah had blamed her. It wasn't fair. She was wrestling with her own problems. Couldn't her daughter see that?

It had been so easy to withdraw, to shut out the voices and fall back into sherry-fueled reveries. To bask in old memories, Hannah's first tooth, her first day at school, passing her fifty-meter swimming certificate, getting chicken pox, making dinner—cucumber strips and hummus—and *Ribena* cartons. Memories bleached white with use, but Ami was still re-living them, was re-living them now, one for each breathless step she took up to the other daughter's room.

Supposedly, before you died your life flashed before you, but Hannah's had latched on to her instead. Beating time through the homely slide-show was the insistent *thump-crump, thump-crump* of new Hannah's music getting louder and louder.

At the top of the stairs Ami turned on old Hannah. Her daughter had the scissors held blades up. How many times had she told her? When you're walking in the house, *blades down*. They looked like a divining rod, leading the way up to the troll's den. Maybe it was the iron, some magical property inherent in the metal. Maybe it was the hungry look in Hannah's eyes.

"How do I know it's not you?" Ami said.

"What?"

"How do I know you're not the changeling? That you're not trying to trick me?"

"That's absurd," Hannah said.

"Is it?"

Hannah tried to step around her. Ami blocked her way.

"Why have you come back now, Hannah?"

"What is this? What are you saying, Mum?"

"We weren't happy exactly, but we were getting by, taking each day as it comes. Then you turn up, looking like *this*, picking the scabs off old wounds, raking through the embers. You had no right. So I ask you, how do I know it's not you?"

The girl changed. She did, right then and there. There was a perceptible *hardening*. What more proof was needed?

"Get out of my way, Mum," she said.

"No."

Then they were together again, after so many months apart. Close enough to smell her hair. It was as fresh as corn marigolds. The real Hannah, she'd never have let her mother hug her, not like this, and maybe this one struggled, too, but only a little. She yielded beneath a wave of unconditional love, especially when Ami turned her wrist. Turning, and turning, and *twisting*, until the closed blades came down, down, down. How many times, young lady? *Safety first.*

Afterward, Ami wiped her hands on her apron. She cleared her throat and knocked on Hannah's door. She had to knock three times, like a scene from a fairy tale and on the third she gave up the suffering-mother act and pushed the door inward. The noise struck her an almost physical blow, jarring her teeth like rocks in a tumbler. Then the sickening stench washed over her. Last to hit home was the sight of Hannah and Gerp—or Goik—sitting together on the end of the unmade bed. Their backs were to Ami, their faces inclined toward one other.

Hannah saw Ami out of the corner of her eye. She reared up and away from Gerp, wiping the back of her hand across her mouth.

"Mum! For Christ's sake, how many times do I have to tell you to bloody knock!"

*Look at her*, Ami thought. She doesn't need all that foundation. And why does she have to wear her hair like that? All those lovely golden locks lopped off and the left-over thatch spiked with gunk. It makes her look so *angry*.

"Earth to Mum? Are you off your pills or what?"

Ami tried to smile. "I did knock, but you didn't hear me because the music's too loud. Can you turn it down a bit? I can't hear myself think down there."

The room looked like a tornado had hit it, dirty clothes and dust, like a new stratum of the earth's crust. Gerp's rolling kit was spread out on the dressing table. Tobacco-ants flecked the pine surface. Gerp himself was still sitting on the bed. He was tidying himself up. Licking his fingers maybe, though it was hard to be sure with his face obscured by all that greasy seaweed-hair. The most Ami ever got out of him was an *Ullo, Mrs. Hairsine.* He'd never once met her eye.

Hannah harrumphed, and then yelled, "Oh fer God's sake!" as she stomped over to the iPod. She notched the volume down an almost imperceptible level or two. "*There*, okay?"

"Thanks, luv. Just one other thing."

Hannah scowled. "What?"

"I just—I just wanted to tell you how much I loved you. That's all."

Hannah grimaced. Gerp snickered.

Ami exited the grisly tableau. She closed the door gently behind her. The music immediately went back up at least three notches. She went down the corridor to where Hannah—the other Hannah—was bunched crookedly by the wall. She leaned down and tenderly scooped a lock of hair from her freckled face. Then she picked up the pair of scissors from where they had fallen and turned back toward her other daughter's room.

There'd been a second, just a second, before Hannah had spotted Ami. She'd jumped up, and Gerp had hastily tucked something under the bed. Ami had seen it all the same. They'd been enjoying it together, side by side, passing it between them, ripping chunks off with their teeth, passing it on, back and forth, like it was a special treat, a shared experience as intimate as a kiss.

It was a tattered badger carcass. You could even pick out the tire-tread, the lazy little monsters.

Ami tried to keep her gorge down. She felt the coolness of the iron in her hand, allowed it harden her resolve. The scissors led the way.

# OLD AND IN THE WAY
*by Wayne Faust*

November is a cruel month in the valley. The bright leaves of October turn to brown mulch underfoot. Fog invades with deathlike fingers, covering rockrose and stitchwort alike with hoary frost. When you can see it at all, the sun barely hovers above the dark, looming mountains.

In a chilly bedroom on the second floor of a moribund manor house lay a very old man. He was sprawled upon an ancient feather bed, his granite face illuminated by the light of a single, flickering candle. His eyes were shut, and his breath came in rasps. His body was crushed by threadbare blankets, torn sheets, and the weight of ninety-three years of hard living. Those years had contained more adventures than most mortals experience in a hundred lifetimes. All of that was past and forgotten, forgotten by everyone but him. Ten years ago he had still been amazingly vital, defying decay in all its forms. Now it was November, and decay had settled in for good.

"Wake up, Uncle," a woman said, shaking him. "I brought you tea."

He opened his rheumy eyes. He knew that voice. It was his grandniece, named after…whom? His daughter? No, he had only one child, a son, long dead. His wife? No, she was dead as well after years in an asylum from grief over their son's death.

The woman spoke again. "Lord knows, I should be the one who sleeps all the time with what I have to do to take care of you. Listening to your crazy stories, the same ones, over, and over, and over. Or should I call them fairy tales? Because that's what they are. Then having to wipe your arse every day and night. And for what? It's not like you'll ever get well."

Then he remembered her name and whom she had been named after. "Mina!" he croaked. His eyes darted toward the window where the fog outside swirled in an opaque, gray mass. "Almost dark!" he exclaimed, trying to sit up.

Mina stifled a yawn and eased him back down. "Yes, yes, Uncle, it's almost dark, and you're afraid of the dark. Just like a little boy. I'm already raising two little boys, and I don't need a third. Besides, we have electricity these days, unlike when you were young, and they needed torches and lanterns."

Through the floor the old man heard the sound of running feet and the clomping of wooden toys from the parlor below.

"How long have I been out?" he pleaded.

She sighed heavily. "I don't know. Three or four days this time."

"Three or four *days*?" He again tried to sit up but his emaciated arms had no strength. "What is the date?" he asked.

Mina clucked. "Always the same question when you wake up. What is the date? As if that should make any difference to you. All you do is lie here day after day. Well, if you must know, it's the eighteenth of November."

"*Mein Gott*," the old man muttered. He knew the calendar and phases of the moon better than anyone alive. "The boys! Send them up here! You are all in great danger!"

"We're *always* in great danger," hissed Mina. "Every time you wake up. I should have let you sleep this time."

The cold, hard fact was Mina had finally reached her limit. The old man had simply become *too much*. Too many bedpans. Too many sleepless nights. Too many men in her life scared away by her responsibilities to the old fool.

"Here's what I'm going to do, Uncle," she said firmly. "I'm going to do nothing this time. No more hanging garlic. No more crucifixes in the windows. No more all-night vigils. Maybe I'll even leave the windows cracked open so you can hear the *creatures of the night* as you call them. You know what's going to happen then? *Nothing*. Not a single, solitary thing. Tomorrow morning the sun will come up over the mountains, and you'll realize what a senile old fool you are. Maybe your heart won't be able to stand the stress, and it will finally stop beating, and at long last, I'll have a life."

The old man gaped. Mina had been talking like this for a while now, but clearly she was serious this time. He was more afraid than he had ever been, not for himself but for the two little boys playing downstairs, Gerhard, ten years old, and little Ben. He loved them dearly, and they still believed. Either one of them could carry on the work if only given more time to learn, but his work was not for little boys. He simply *had* to stay alive long enough to teach them. They carried his blood in their veins after all.

"Mina, please," the old man pleaded, his face growing beet red as he again tried to raise himself up.

Mina simply laughed as she pushed him down again, a little harder this time. "I'm glad I took Karl's name, even though he walked out on us after you scared him off," she declared, her eyes flashing defiance. "I'm a Zimmerman now. I'll never be a *Van Helsing* again! Once you're gone, that name will vanish forever into old and moldy books of scary stories."

Before the old man could sputter a reply, she stomped out of the room, slamming the door behind her. He heard whispers from outside the window. He had been at it long enough to know there were things out there. They had begun to move, or were they waiting, still frightened of him? Did they know how weak he had become?

He felt a wild thumping in his chest and a fierce pain, radiating into his left arm. He clutched his arms tightly to himself. "No!" he gasped. In his mind he was already downstairs protecting the house. Protecting the children, the way he had done for so many over his long years.

He had fought a solitary crusade, overcoming bone-crushing weariness, skepticism, and the enemy. Always the enemy. Creatures unimaginable except in the worst nightmares, but these were not nightmares. They were real as flesh and blood—undead flesh and undead blood preying on innocents like the precious boys downstairs.

He sensed the night coming on and the full moon rising. It motivated him to use his last ounce of fading energy. He rolled out from beneath the covers and tried to swing his legs around. Instead, he tumbled out of bed and onto the wooden floor with a thud. All the air left his lungs, but he still managed to crawl toward the door, eyes wide, drool leaking from one side of his mouth, skeletal fingers scraping against old planking. He pulled himself forward, one agonizing inch at a time, head up, eyes focused on the sliver of light at the bottom of the door to the hallway. He had fought so many battles. So many. Surely he could do it just one more time. Surely he could overcome his own frailties. The lives of those two boys depended on him making it downstairs.

It was not to be. His breath simply ran out. His head flopped down to the floor. His eyes closed. His hands were still poised on the floorboards like claws but they were no longer pulling him forward. He let out one final wheeze, and his chest went rigid. A tendril of mist trickled past his now dead lips and ascended up toward the ceiling. His skin grew cold and hard as granite.

Outside the manor house, the fog swirled round and round, blocking out stars and electric lights alike. As the night fell hard upon the land, a whole symphony of beastly sounds echoed through the high, dark mountains. Moments later, an army of long-frustrated creatures crept forward into the valley, unopposed at last.

# About Our Authors

V. E. Battaglia was born on Long Island, New York in 1988. His first foray into publication was at age twelve when his poetry was featured in a special edition of *Newsday*. He now primarily writes Science Fiction and Horror. His work can be found in the *Zen of the Dead* anthology from Popcorn Press and in the *SNAFU: Hunters* anthology from Cohesion Press. He currently resides in New York with his two cats.

Adam L. Bealby writes weird fiction, leaning heavily into fantasy, horror, and arch satire. He dabbles in stories for children, too. His short stories and comic work have been published in numerous anthologies, including *Spooked* (Bridge House Publishing), *Dragontales* (Wyvern Publishing), *Pagan* (Zimbell House Publishing), *Darkness Abound* (Migla Press) and *Murky Depths* magazine. He lives in Worcestershire with his wife, three children, and a harried imagination. Catch up with his latest ravings on Twitter @adamskilad.

Chantal Boudreau is an accountant/author/illustrator who lives in Nova Scotia, Canada with her husband and two children. An affiliate member of the Horror Writers Association, she writes and illustrates horror, steampunk, sci-fi, dark fantasy, and fantasy and has had dozens of her stories published in a variety of anthologies, online journals, and magazines. Her novels include *Fervor*, a dystopian series, and *Masters & Renegades*, a fantasy series. Find out more at: chantellyb.wordpress.com.

Wayne Faust has been a full time music and comedy performer for over forty years. While on the road performing he also writes fiction. He's had more than 40 stories published in various anthologies and magazines in Australia, South Africa, Norway, and England. He's also published two complete books. He's a busy guy. You can find everything you need to know about Wayne's show and writing on his website at WayneFaust.com.

৵✄ॐ

Charles Frierman lives in Florida with his beautiful wife and twelve—yes twelve—pets. By day, he works as a children's storyteller at the local library, but writing has always been his passion. Ever since he was a little kid, he has been trying to put words to paper, but he never had the confidence to pursue it further, until recently.

৵✄ॐ

Laurel Anne Hill's award-winning novel, *Heroes Arise*, was published by KOMENAR in 2007. Her published short stories and nonfiction pieces total forty and have appeared most recently in *Fault Zone*, *A Bard Day's Knight*, *Horror Addicts Guide to Life*, and *Shanghai Steam*. *Shanghai Steam*, nominated for an Aurora Award in 2013, is recommended by *Writing Fantasy & Science Fiction*. Laurel has served as a writing workshop mentor and/or panelist at many science fiction/fantasy conventions. She's the Literary Stage Manager for the annual San Mateo County Fair in California, a writing contest judge, and a proofreader/editor. Visit LaurelAnneHill.com for more information.

Nickie Jamison wrote her first full-length novel at age ten. That creative endeavor sparked her desire to begin her writing career. Her short erotic fiction has been published in the *Coming Together Among the Stars*, *Coming Together Outside the Box*, and *Coming Together Strange Shifters* anthologies. Nickie's hobbies include knitting, drinking copious amounts of wine, Netflix binge-watching, and painting her nails. She lives in Hampton Roads with her darling husband, step-child, and two spoiled furbabies, Jayne and Frye.

❧✄❧

C.S. Kane is a dark fiction author. Her debut novella, *Shattered*, was released by *DarkFuse* in 2013 and garnered many positive reviews with *Black Static Magazine* stating "The author has talent." Kane has written many features, reviews, and articles on a wide variety of horror related topics for *Dark Media Online*. She has previously promoted the genre at large events like TitanCon and is active within the community through contributions to initiatives such as Women in Horror Month. You can find the author on Facebook: CSKane13, Twitter @CS_Kane, or via the website CSKane.com.

❧✄❧

A fan of all things fantastical and frightening, Shannon Lawrence writes primarily horror and fantasy. Her stories can be found in several anthologies and magazines, including *The Deep Dark Woods, Under the Bed*, and *Devolution Z*. When she's not writing, she's hiking through the wilds of Colorado and photographing her magnificent surroundings. Though she often misses the ocean, the majestic and rugged Rockies are a sight she could never part with. Besides, in Colorado there's always a place to hide a body or birth a monster. What more could she ask for? Find her at TheWarriorMuse.com.

Sara E. Lundberg is a writer and freelance editor from Kansas. She writes and edits primarily fantasy and horror. Her short stories have appeared in the anthologies *Shadows of the Mind* and *Misunderstood*, online at the Rose Red Review, and she has won both third place and honorable mention in the Writers Weekly 24-hour Short Story contest. Sara is also an editor and contributor for the Confabulator Cafe, her writing group's website, where they write new short stories every month. You can find her online at SELundberg.com.

∽✄∾

MD Maurice has been publishing erotica and mainstream fiction since early 2001. She has been previously published in several anthologies, Leucrotia Press's *Abaculus III* science fiction and horror anthology, and by Rainstorm Press in their *Nailed—An Erotic Death Anthology*. She has also had her work featured on Oysters and Chocolate, Erotic Nights, and Erotic Shades websites. *River Poet's Journal* and *Dark Gothic Resurrected* magazines have also recently published some of her fiction. MD is a regular contributor and co-founder of a group, Sensual Infusions at Writing.com where she mentors newbie authors pursuing publication.

∽✄∾

Alison McBain lives in Connecticut with her husband and three daughters. She has over thirty publications in magazines and anthologies, including *Flash Fiction Online*, *Abyss & Apex*, and *Frozen Fairy Tales* (World Weaver Press). When not obsessing over who's going to bite the big one on *The Walking Dead*, she practices origami meditation and draws all over the walls of her house with the enthusiastic help of her kids. You can read her blog at AlisonMcBain.com or chat with her on Twitter @AlisonMcBain.

Lynn McSweeney has written short stories and poems all her life. Having retired early, she now has the time to burnish each tale and brave the untested waters of publishing. A childhood spent traveling meant eleven schools by ninth grade, including a two-room schoolhouse in rural Ireland. She has worked—for fun, pay, or both—as an illustrator, muralist, minister, off-set printer, Madison Avenue font-embellisher (pre-computer), legal secretary, grass-roots organizer, and stay-at-home mother.

❧✂❧

Emerian Rich is the author of the vampire book series, *Night's Knights*. Her most recent full length novel, *Artistic License*, is about a woman who inherits a house, where anything she paints on the walls comes alive. She's been published in a handful of anthologies by publishers such as Dragon Moon Press, Hidden Thoughts Press, Hazardous Press, and White Wolf Press. Emerian is the podcast horror hostess of HorrorAddicts.net.

❧✂❧

Dan Shaurette is a goth-geek from Phoenix, AZ. He has been a fan of horror—especially vampires—ever since seeing Bela Lugosi's *Dracula* as a young child. He has been published in *An Improbable Truth: The Paranormal Adventures of Sherlock Holmes* (Mocha Memoirs Press), *Fresh Blood* (Vampire Writers Support Group), *Horrible Disasters* (HorrorAddicts.net), and *Horror Addicts Guide to Life* (HorrorAddicts.net). Please check out HorrorAddicts.net where you can listen to his serialized stories, *Black Magic* and *Black Jack*, or visit MattBlackBooks.com.

J. Malcolm Stewart is a Northern California-based author and journalist, with over twenty short fiction publications to his name. He spends most of his weekends talking about how to not be in a real-life horror movie.

❧ ✕ ❦

DJ Tyrer is the person behind Atlantean Publishing and has been widely published in anthologies and magazines in the UK, USA, and elsewhere, including *Chilling Horror Short Stories* (Flame Tree), *State of Horror: Illinois* (Charon Coin Press), *Steampunk Cthulhu* (Chaosium), *Tales of the Black Arts* (Hazardous Press), *Ill-considered Expeditions* (April Moon Books), and *Sorcery & Sanctity: A Homage to Arthur Machen* (Hieroglyphics Press), and in addition, has a novella available in paperback and on the Kindle, *The Yellow House* (Dunhams Manor). To find out more, visit DJTyrer.blogspot.co.uk or AtlanteanPublishing.blogspot.co.uk.

❧ ✕ ❦

"Briar" is K.L. Wallis' first publication. She resides on the Sunshine Coast, Australia, and is undertaking post-graduate studies in creative writing at the University of the Sunshine Coast. Although born and raised in Australia, she finds much of her inspiration stems from her Bavarian ancestry. She writes a range of genres including magical realism, gothic fiction, high fantasy, mythological fiction, and contemporary folk-lore. She is also the owner/editor of Restricted Quill—a small editing company she operates with her fiancé. Restricted Quill can be found on Facebook and at RestrictedQuill.wordpress.com.

# Horror Addicts Guide to Life

Do you love the horror genre? Do you look at horror as a
lifestyle? Do the "norms" not understand your love of the
macabre?
Despair no longer, my friend, for within your grasp is a
book written by those who look at horror as a way of life,
just like you. This is your guide to living a horrifying
existence. Featuring interviews with Midnight Syndicate,
Valentine Wolfe, and The Gothic Tea Society.

## the wickeds

HorrorAddicts.net presents thirteen horror tales from up-
and-coming women writers. This diverse collection of
revenge, torture, and macabre is sure to quench any horror
addict's thirst for blood. Between these covers reside
werewolves, demons, ghosts, vampires, a voodoo priestess,
headless horseman, Bloody Mary, and human monsters who
are perhaps the most disturbing. All proceeds will be
donated to LitWorld, a non-profit organization that uses the
power of story to cultivate literacy leaders around the globe.

## HORRIBLE DISASTERS

HorrorAddicts.net proudly presents, *Horrible Disasters*.
Thirteen authors from around the globe share their visions
of terror set during real natural disasters throughout history.
Travel back in time to earth shattering events like the
eruption of Mount Vesuvius in 79 A.D., the San Francisco
earthquake of 1906, and the Winter of Terror avalanches,
1950. What supernatural events went unnoticed? What
creatures caused such destruction without remorse? Stock
your emergency kit, hunker in your bunker, and prepare
for…*Horrible Disasters*. Proceeds go to help disaster relief
globally by way of the Rescue Task Force.

# HorrorAddicts.net

Do you love horror?
Want to hear a podcast created by
horror fanatics just like you?
Listen to HorrorAddicts.net.

Real horror reported by real horror fans.
We cover the news and reviews of horror:

☠movies     ☠games     ☠books
☠manga     ☠anime     ☠music
☠comics     ☠locations     ☠events
☠rpgs     ☠fashion     ☠more!

Every episode features horror authors, podcasters, movie
people, musicians, and horror personalities.

Featuring the annual Wicked Women Writer's Challenge,
Masters of Macabre Contest, and Writer's Workshop
Competition.

*for* Horror Addicts, *by* Horror Addicts.
Your one stop horror source:

# HorrorAddicts.net

HorrorAddicts.net

33185710R00157

Made in the USA
San Bernardino, CA
26 April 2016